THE MISADVENTURES OF

MAESTRO MAXIMILIAN

DAMIEN MICHAEL SHINDELMAN

authorHOUSE®

AuthorHouse™
1663 Liberty Drive
Bloomington, IN 47403
www.authorhouse.com
Phone: 833-262-8899

Published by AuthorHouse 11/28/2020

ISBN: 978-1-6655-0891-9 (sc)
ISBN: 978-1-6655-0889-6 (hc)
ISBN: 978-1-6655-0890-2 (e)

Library of Congress Control Number: 2020923851

Print information available on the last page.

FOREWORD

I wrestled over the subject matter of this book for the past seven years.

This was my first attempt at dark comedy, and I labored to find a happy medium between what was funny in a satirical way, yet not glorifying outright blood and gore. Since the majority of characters in my tale are mobsters, counterfeiters, corrupt law enforcement officers, prison inmates, a few symphonic musicians, and one orchestra conductor, it was difficult to avoid some of the more sordid aspects of the people's unusual lives and careers. As vengeful and violent as some of the characters tend to behave, I also tried to show their human side whenever possible.

The portrayals of violence in various scenes were used to define the characters lack of civility and twisted desires that most people will assume are part of the organized crime world. In no way was I trying to condone violence of any kind. I believe, if you can get dark comedy right, one should smirk at the absurdity of the characters and their woefully skewed lives. The intricate and devious methods they use to dispose of their enemies is simply icing on the cake.

The old adage, "what goes around comes around," is an

important theme in my book. I am sure you will agree that it is an insightful maxim that we all have experienced throughout our lives. I truly hope you enjoy the ironic twists and woefully flawed characters I have portrayed.

Now grab my book and a glass of wine, then find a comfy reading spot.

Let the games begin!

Damien Michael Shindelman

CHAPTER 1
THE SCAM

It was well past 2AM, and Zane Worth was still working tirelessly at his color printer.

After months of refinement, the bogus bill looked remarkable, but the finicky counterfeiter was still not satisfied. The myriad of intricate details and complex hues were nearly perfect, but the background paper was not an exact match. Then, there was that exasperating coded strip embedded within the document. That irritating detail had been an almost insurmountable problem.

He took a moment to curse the US Treasury Department, and quickly returned to his work. Adding the different flecks of color on the paper from the real bill details on his computer screen, he copied the results along with the problematic black strip onto a blank bill. Encouraged by the results, he printed over the blank with the rest of the one-hundred-dollar scrolling. After scanning over the final result carefully, a shrewd smile broke out over his face.

The Ben Franklin looked first-rate, yet conspicuously unused. However, after a pass through the washing machine and some quick ironing, Zane was sure that the bills would fool most

1

unsuspecting people. He saved the finished document on his computer hard drive and printed a thousand copies, changing the serial numbers after every ten bills. Once he had generated one-hundred-thousand dollars, he carefully trimmed the forgeries and let them cure under a black light.

Well aware that one had to be extremely careful when passing on counterfeit currency; Zane had formulated a scheme to remain safe from detection.

When spending bogus money, he knew that most people's biggest mistake was greed.

Some impatient numbskulls used the phony cash to buy high-ticket items like cars or jewelry but were quickly caught by experienced shop owners who knew have the bills checked before the sale was finalized.

An even worse idea was to try and pass off the fraudulent cash at a casino. Even the most exhausted blackjack dealer could spot a fake Franklin in a nano second. Zane knew, once you were escorted to a back room and the casino goons had done their worst, they would then turn you into the Feds, extremely bruised and bloodied. Zane felt far too clever to make a boneheaded blunder like that.

Mr. Worth had decided to go into the pharmaceutical business. He had met with an underworld contact at the local strip bar and had placed an order for a hundred grands worth of pure, uncut cocaine.

His plan was simple. After purchasing the drugs with his phony notes, he would cut it, package it, and then sell the junk on the street. He figured he could quadruple his investment and have real cash to boot. He assumed that the high-quality fake bills would most likely go undeleted by the drug cartel runner and would quickly be laundered by shady foreign banks.

If his contact didn't examine the loot with a fine-toothed comb, Zane figured he was sitting on easy street.

The night of the drug transaction, Zane carefully packed the ersatz bills into a suitcase. He placed real one-hundred's on the top of each stack just in case the seller might use a chemical pen to check for fakes. With his stomach tied in knots, he didn't want to think about what would happen to him if he was caught red-handed trying to pass off the tainted currency to the mob.

Zane drove to the rendezvous site; a seedy hotel located in a heavily blighted section of Queens.

Following his contact's instructions, he had rented a rundown, roach infested cubicle for an hour. Once inside the grimy room, he placed the briefcase on a table visible through the front window, then sat on the bed. A few minutes later, there was a sharp rap on the door. With his heart pounding wildly, Zane opened the door and the man from the strip club walked in carrying a medium sized satchel.

Without uttering a word, the short and rotund stranger placed the briefcase on the bed next to Zane and opened the latches. Inside were ten individual packages, each containing a brick of cocaine. Zane cut open one of the bags and scraped off a bit to taste. Not being completely unfamiliar with the substance, Zane immediately knew he had a fortune in unadulterated drugs sitting next to him.

When the forger nodded his head in approval, the sinister contact opened Zane's suitcase, quickly flipping through the stacks of money. Returning the head gesture with a grim smile, the underworld goon grabbed the cash, then quickly disappeared into the night.

Zane sat motionless on the bed for several minutes, his brain awash in relief. He couldn't believe how easily the deal had gone down.

Grabbing the briefcase, he exited the room, then made a hasty retreat to his car. Once safely inside, he gunned the motor and raced back to his place. After flinging open his apartment door in a rush, he quickly locked himself inside.

As he started cutting down the first white block, his brain was already formulating plans as to how he was going to spend the money. With genuine cash in hand, he was going to go on a shopping spree, followed by a trip to the BMW dealership. He was tired of living like a bum, and knew that his ship had finally come in.

Eventually growing weary from the evening's excitement, Zane barricaded the front door with a chair and made his way to the bedroom. He quickly fell asleep with grandiose visions of the high life swirling inside in his spent brain.

The next morning, Zane finished preparing a batch of eight balls, and called some of his user friends to see if they would be interested in a buy. To obtain a name for himself as the premier cocaine dealer in the area, Zane had purposely cut the pure cocaine by fifty percent, knowing that the highly euphoric effect would still be most stimulating to his buyers.

Within the hour, one of his pals had dropped in, excited at the news of scoring some primo Colombian nose candy.

They sat at the kitchen table, first carefully stacking lines of power on a mirror, then snorting the highly potent drug with one of Zane's bogus bills. The effect was instantaneous, and both men were instantly sent reeling from the exhilarating rush. After the second hit, his high-flying friend threw down three grand to buy all that he had prepared that morning.

Feeling completely invincible, Zane sent his buyer packing so he could start preparing additional product to sell.

By late afternoon, he had produced another ten grands' worth of blow. His plan was to visit the most popular night spots and bars in Manhattan. Once the word had spread about the primo crazy dust, he was convinced he could peddle his entire stash within a few hours.

After checking out his dismal reflection in the mirror, he realized that first thing on his agenda was to purchase some better-looking duds. After all, anyone hanging out at a high-class establishment wasn't going to be interested in buying anything from a dealer dressed like a bedraggled street person.

He pocketed his friend's cash and sauntered outside, cheerfully hopping into his late model Buick without a care in the world.

At the mall, he requested some help from a well-dressed clerk, claiming he had no idea what was in style these days. In less than twenty minutes, Zane was looking at an entirely new man reflected in the mirror.

He was astonished to see at how well he had cleaned up. With his formfitting suit, wavy black hair and transparent blue eyes, Zane thought he looked like a trendy Esquire model. Thoroughly pleased with his transformation, he tipped the clerk a fifty and walked brashly out the door.

Gussied-up in his black silk Italian suit, Gucci loafers, and skintight crimson shirt, Zane strode confidently into the swankiest bar in mid-town called *Cloud 9*.

He knew this was the spot where the cream of well-healed New York society came to let their hair down and mingle in a highly charged atmosphere. Ignoring the block long line of anxious guests waiting to enter, Zane casually flashed five hundred dollars at the bouncer, who palmed the cash and let him walk right in.

Once inside, he casually surveyed the dance floor looking for potential customers, knowing perfectly well that blow heads were easy to spot. Young or old, fat or thin, there was one sign that gave the highly conspicuous group away. Zane was searching for highly energized patrons who kept fussing with their noses as they left the lavatory.

A middle-aged woman dressed in flashy designer couture exited the ladies' room with an exuberant smile radiating over her face. Looking a bit disoriented, she clumsily made her way back to the bar. Zane moseyed in her direction, deftly finding a stool a few feet away. As she ordered a Cosmo from the bar tender, he furtively glanced at her nose. Zane smiled upon seeing the telltale sign of white powder ringing her nostrils.

After polite introductions, they chatted for a few minutes. When the mood felt right, Zane asked if she would be interested in trying a few lines. Without a moment's hesitation, the woman grabbed Zane's hand, leading him to a dimly lit room in the back of the establishment. After Zane passed her a small sample, she pulled out a cosmetic mirror and divvied out a few lines. Within minutes of snorting the dizzy dust, the highly impressed woman pulled out a grand from her purse, then hurriedly stashed the coke.

Like wildfire, word had spread throughout the bar about the fabulous *Bump,* and Zane had quickly sold out his entire batch. With tens of thousands in cash in his pocket, he blessed Lady luck and strode confidently to his beat-up clunker parked in the side alley.

Unlocking the door, he slid into the driver's seat, still gloating over his financial windfall. As he reached to turn the key, he noticed a piece of paper attached to his windshield wiper. With his curiosity aroused, he got back out of the vehicle and pulled the mysterious item from the blade. To his alarm, it was one of his bogus bills bearing a simple message.

"You're a dead man," was scrawled out, and under the threatening message was a sketch of an unhappy face.

The dire message put Zane in panic mode. Jumping back into his car, he floored it out of the alley way. In his overzealous attempt to flee the bar, he came within inches of broad siding several passing motorists.

As he raced haphazardly down the street, Zane's mind whirled with fear.

Someone was on to him, and he wondered if it was the underworld contact who had sold him the coke. He assumed that the surly courier had discovered that most all of the cash was bogus and was now out for revenge.

Then, an even worse thought crossed his mind. The threat could also be the work of a drug cartel assassin or pissed-off mob boss since he had no idea where the uncut cocaine had originated. Zane sped home like a man possessed, screeching to a stop in front of his apartment. He flew out of the car and up the three flights of stairs to his room, then slammed the door behind him.

Trying to catch his breath, he grabbed a duffel bag and threw his stash of bump inside. Without missing a beat, Zane opened the bedroom window and climbed down the fire escape. He figured, if someone was watching his car from the street, he could slip away unobserved.

Carefully looking around to see if anyone was watching, he ran down the alley to the next block and hailed a cab. Desperate to get out the city as fast as humanly possible, Zane ordered the driver to head for New Jersey.

As he passed over the George Washington Bridge, Zane started to slowly relax.

He had been staring out the rear windshield for most of the

trip and realized that no one seemed to be following him. Not exactly sure of his next move, Zane had the cab driver drop him off at a park by the river.

Still dressed in his snazzy club wear, he knew he stood out like a sore thumb. Even the bums were giving him a wary eye, not sure if they should try to beg for spare change, or just mind their own business.

"The first thing I should have done after passing the fake bills was to get the hell out of Manhattan," he thought regretfully.

After spending months of planning, Zane started to kick himself for not thinking that this possible situation might arise. No matter what, he knew that he had to flee from the East Coast as quickly as possible. Not exactly sure how he was going to make his escape; the panicked forger grabbed his bag and started walking toward the hazy lights of Newark.

As he got closer to town, Zane saw a rundown used car lot with a glaring neon sign flashing *Open 24 hours.* He entered the office and woke up a ratty looking man who was snoozing away on grease stained couch in the corner.

"How can I help you, Mr. Fancy Pants?" the snarky auto broker questioned.

Zane said he was looking for a dependable commuter car for around fifteen-hundred bucks.

The clerk led him outside, and after fifteen minutes of haggling, they had made a deal on a well-worn 81' Dodge Caravan. After paying the man in cash, Zane asked if he could throw in an US atlas.

Once he had placed his signature on the dotted line, Zane started-up the aging vehicle and headed toward I- 295 south. Connecting with I-95, he drove all night, ending up in Stoney Creek, Virginia. Exhausted from the traumatic events of the day, he pulled off the road at a rest stop. After checking all the door locks, he fell fast asleep curled up in the back of the van.

Six hours later, Zane awoke refreshed and ready to roll.

He stretched his arms and legs lazily, then slowly crawled back into the driver's seat.

After having a brain storm in the middle of the night, he planned on heading to a small southern Arizona town called Tombstone. The name sounded slightly morose, but he was sure he could hide out easily in the remote desert hamlet for an extended period of time. Opened the atlas, he started going over several different routes that would lead him toward his destination.

As Zane started the motor, he laughed nervously, then shouted out, *"Go west, young man!"* Feeling a tad more secure about his future, he gave a big *"Yee Haw"* and started to pull out of his parking space.

After glancing out the driver side window, he slammed on the brakes. Traced in the grimy road film was a message.

"Where in hell do you think you're going?" Below the note was another disturbing unhappy face, glaring at him with evil intent.

Instantly panicking, Zane took off with the tires smoking, and peeled onto the freeway. Out of his mind with fear, he shrieked, *"Crap! Now what do I do?"* Blinded with fear, he drove down the freeway like a madman, weaving across lanes. Passing car after car, Zane kept screaming like Lucifer's pitchfork was jabbing at his backside.

Cursing at the blinking gas gauge light, Zane pulled into a busy filling station, parking where he saw a lot of other travelers hanging out.

"Whoever is stalking me won't have the nerve to try anything with people around," he nervously surmised. He filled up the van,

bought some junk food, and then returned to the vehicle. After scouring over his maps for an hour, Zane believed he had devised a foolproof plan to elude his unknown pursuer.

The cowering counterfeiter waited until dark before slowly pulling out of the Minimart.

He looked about carefully for anyone who might be following him. Seeing nothing out of the ordinary, he took the next exit and started to drive down a small side hi-way. He reconnected with the interstate and headed north, hoping his misdirection would throw off his tail.

After driving for 20 minutes, he turned off his lights and crossed back over the median, heading back on the south bound interstate once more. In North Carolina, he took I-40, and headed west. So far, there had been no sign of anyone following him and he gradually started to realize he had finally ditched his hunter.

Approaching the outskirts of Knoxville, he pulled into a sprawling truck stop. With his vehicle well known to his tail, Zane had decided to ditch the van and catch a ride.

Grabbing his bag, he entered the café, strategically picking a stool next to the register. He quietly listened in on each trucker's conversation with the cashier, hoping to overhear of someone heading in his direction.

While sipping at his coffee, Zane focused his attention on a large, brusque, female driver. She was making a course joke about hauling a load of toilet paper to Phoenix. Sounding perfect for his plan, Zane put on the charm and secured a ride with the gregarious older woman.

After finalizing the travel arrangements, Zane purchased some tee shirts, jeans, baseball cap, and sunglasses at the gift shop. In the restroom, he changed into his touristy disguise, stuffing his hair inside his hat. Throwing on his shades, he walked calmy out the back door and met up with the driver next to her pink Mack rig.

"Name's Pat," the husky trucker said as she reached out to shake his hand. Zane nodded, introducing himself as they climbed into the cab.

"This is going to be a long haul. I hope you know how to entertain an old gal like me along the way," she growled.

At this point, Zane didn't care if he had to hump a gorilla to get away from his stalker.

"Pat, I'll ride ya' all the way to Arizona, and show you all the sights of interest on the way," he quipped back good-naturedly.

With a hearty laugh, Pat pulled out of the truck stop, giving two long honks on the horn. *"That's for good luck,"* she blurted out with a toothy grin.

"Great, 'cause I could use a ton of that right now," Zane sighed to himself.

They drove all day, only stopping on occasion to weigh-in the truck. As the mismatched duo rolled their way west, the trucker chattered nonstop.

Zane was highly relieved when Pat confessed that she was not interested in men what-so-ever. He learned that she lived with her life partner in Globe and drove truck because traveling the country was her life's passion.

Zane let her do most of the talking; only chiming in when she questioned him directly. He felt it might not be wise to give out a lot of information about himself, just in case she accidentally started blabbing to the wrong people.

In a quieter moment, Pat turned to Zane with a questioning look. *"Tell me my elusive friend; what are you running away from?"*

Flabbergasted by Pat's insight, Zane's face openly gave away his guilt. After going over all the crazy details of the past two days, Pat stared at her passenger with a look of complete disbelief.

"Sounds like you stepped into a huge pile of crap," Pat huffed amusedly. All Zane could do was nod in agreement, somewhat embarrassed by the truth.

"Now, don't you go worrying about it my friend. We've all made a few mistakes in our lives," Pat said with a smirk. *"Rest assured, you're safe with me. I promise you; nobody messes with this mean old bitch!"*

Pat's quip made them both laugh for several minutes, with tears of mirth starting to pour down the trucker's ruddy cheeks. After she had settled down, Pat turned to Zane wearing a sincere expression. *"Don't sweat it kid; by the time I get you to Arizona, your stalker will be long gone."*

At 10PM, Pat pulled the big rig off the road. *"That's all I can drive today without the highway patrol writing me up,"* she complained.

After performing a list of safety checks, she climbed back inside the cab and disappeared into the upper compartment. After hearing the hum of a micro wave oven, Pat returned with two plates loaded with steaming hot burritos and a proud smile.

"My gal made these, so enjoy. It's the best Mexican food this side of the Mississippi."

The two wolfed down their meals like there was no tomorrow. As they scraped their plates clean, Zane asked about the sleeping situation, with Pat chucking amusedly.

"We can sleep together if you think you're man enough!"

When his face started to flush, Zane smiled sheepishly and said he would be happy to bunk down in the cab.

"No way, my handsome fugitive. You take the upper berth, and

*I will sleep across the cabs seats. Now don't you go worrying over me;
I've done it a million times."*

With the bedding arrangements settled, Zane crawled into the
bunk above the cab, pulling the down-filled comforter over him.
He was eternally grateful that he had met up with the off-color
female trucker. With Pat close by, he finally felt safe and secure.

Before he turned off the cabin light, Zane called out, *"Good
night, Pat."*

A few seconds later, he heard *"Sweet dreams, dumb ass!"* echo
up from the cab below, followed by a hearty guffaw.

Zane awoke with a start, his clothes soaked in cold sweat.

He had been dreaming about the hellbent pursuer and scowling
faces that seemed to be covering everything in sight. No matter
where he ran, or where he hid, he could not escape his diabolical
bloodhound. Exhausted from the chase and unable to breathe, he
felt his life slowly seeping away.

As his mind cleared, Zane calmed down, realizing he was still
safe and sound. When he heard Pat milling about in the cabin
below, he smiled, thinking that if he remained quiet, he could get
another hour of sleep.

Hearing the engine rumble to life, he snuggled back under the
comforter, the drone of the diesel motor quickly lulling him back
into a calming repose.

A few minutes later, Zane was shaken awake by the cab lurching
about violently. It felt like the big rig was on a roller coaster track,
and he was being slammed from one side of the compartment to
the other.

He tried to open the berth door, but it was jammed shut. After what seemed like an eternity, the truck finally came to a dead stop, with the engine idling roughly. After four or five attempts, Zane was finally able to kick open the door and he rushed down to the cab. After flinging open the curtain, he gasped in alarm.

Hogtied to the passenger seat was Pat, gagged and out cold. On her forehead was a crude unhappy face drawn in red magic marker. Across the windshield was a scribbled message, *"No matter how hard you try, you can't lose me!"*

Looking past the threating message, Zane realized that the truck had come to a stop in the middle of a seemly endless cornfield. He turned off the engine and listened intently, not sure if his stalker was waiting outside in ambush.

He searched around the cab for a weapon but found nothing useful to defend himself with. Praying that Pat might have stashed a weapon in the glove box; he grabbed the keys out of the ignition. With his hands trembling spastically, he finally found the one that opened the lock. Reaching inside, Zane felt the cold steel of a firearm.

Grabbing the gun, he quickly checked the clip, finding the weapon was fully loaded.

With his duffel bag slung over his shoulder, he slowly opened the cab door and stepped down into the field with Pat's revolver in hand.

As he crouched by the front tire, all he could see were dense masses of leafy stalks. The tension felt unbearable and he could not stop shaking. Zane was convinced that his maniacal hunter was hiding out in the maze of greenery waiting to butcher him.

CHAPTER 2
LESAL SPURNELL

LESAL SPURNELL HAD BEEN an enforcer for the mob for as long as he could remember.

Being an unusually small yet extremely overweight child, he had been teased mercilessly by all the other children. Quickly becoming both self-conscious and highly defensive, he spent the majority of his early life severely beating any unwise peer who mistakenly crossed him.

Lesal simply adored fighting. During his frequent brawls, he would pin his opponent down on the ground and pound on them ruthlessly. When his victims would beg for him to stop, he would grin from ear to ear, and continue to flail away without mercy.

Discovering that brawling and breaking the law were far more engaging than school work, young Lesal had dropped out at the age of fifteen to begin his lifelong career of crime.

As an adult, the roly-poly mobster was continually mocked by his fellow goons for his short stature and extreme obesity, Lesal had to battle his way up the underworld ladder by proving that he was the toughest, most coldblooded gangster around. By the time he was thirty, even his boss started giving him a wide berth, never quite sure if the repugnant tick might turn on him.

The one passion that Lesal enjoyed most of all was his insatiable fondness for sadism.

When his fellow hoods were sent on a hit, they first located their targets, abducted them, then dragged their ill-fated victims to an isolated spot to dispose of them. To Mr. Spurnell, that tawdry, old school method of murder simply held no interest.

He preferred to stalk his quarry and torture them psychologically during the process. In Lesal's opinion, there was far more entertainment value in tormenting your prey endlessly before you finally wasted them. Like a cat toying with cricket, it was his savory spice of life, and he excelled at intentionally driving his targets totally insane before he finished them off.

At the moment, the hoodlum was on a free-lance job for his own benefit. Earlier in the week he had acted as a courier for his boss, delivering a satchel of uncut cocaine to a strung-out loser he had met in a nudie bar.

He made the drop, collected the cash, and was back at his apartment in less than an hour. After pouring himself a glass of straight whiskey, he had started to count the money to make sure the ledger would balance when he delivered the payola to his boss.

Lesal had almost finished his tally when he noticed that something was slightly fishy about the loot. His eye caught a serial number that he thought he had already seen. Carefully going back over all the bills, he soon realized that there were many duplicate serial numbers in the batch, plus a few genuine bills.

The unexpected discovery got Lesal thinking about a possible money-making scam of his own.

For starters, the counterfeit bills were the best he had ever seen. They would have easily fooled him if he hadn't rechecked the entire lot carefully. As the wheels in his demented brain started spinning, thinking of ways he could take advantage of this unanticipated opportunity, he slowly put his drink down.

Smiling smugly, Lesal restacked and bound all but five of the fake hundreds.

The devious mobster figured if his superior didn't catch the serial number snafu, he wasn't going to say a word. Grabbing the phone, the greedy goon set up an appointment to meet his chief. If the money passed inspection, he was going to find this talented counterfeiter and blackmail him into producing the near perfect fakes for him.

The conniving crook sat quietly as his supervisor, named Axel Gilan, tallied the cash. After finishing the count, *"Seems to be a little short,"* was the only comment made. Looking mildly annoyed, the overworked mob boss added the bogus cash to the rest of the money in the wall vault.

With his assignment completed, Lesal asked Axel if he could take some time off. Feigning a sad look, he pleaded for a vacation to help him unwind. His superior quickly agreed, secretly glad to be rid of the psychotic pariah for an extended period of time. Axel Gilan quickly reached into his desk and pulled out five-grand, quickly tossing the cash to pudgy pugilist.

"Here you go, Mr. Spurnell! Enjoy yourself and take as much time off as you need."

Lesal couldn't have been more pleased. He had been allowed plenty of time to hunt down and intimidate the clueless dolt into doing his bidding.

He figured that the most likely place to locate a blow pusher would be at a trendy dance club or bar. Taking an educated guess, Lesal drove to a joint called *Cloud 9,* thinking that his target might start selling his blow there.

Sure enough, he spied his pusher getting out of his car, then strut cockily into the club, dressed like an 80's disco douche bag.

The mobster waited a few minutes. He then causally walked to the back alley and quickly located his mark's beat-up car. Taking a bogus Franklin from his pocket, the goon wrote his first intimidating message, then signing the note with a menacing scowl.

Lesal Spurnell simply adored the simplistic unhappy caricature. Driven by his all-consuming and understandable fascination, he had collected thousands of items bearing the unpleasant grimace. Much like the creepy vibe most people feel after seeing a circus clown, Lesal knew that his disgruntled logo gave his targets a bad case of the heebie-jeebies. Over time it had become his personal trademark, and if you were ever the recipient of one of his sinister calling cards, you could be sure that you were in "dans la merde."

Knowing his counterfeiter would be in a total panic, Lesal waited in his car until Zane had read the note, then followed him covertly back to his apartment.

From past experience, the mobster realized that most people were unwaveringly set in their ways. If his pigeon had a brain in his body, he should know better than to leave out the front door. Assuming he was correct, the thug had slunk to the alley, casing-out all the windows. A minute later, he saw Zane exit the outside staircase and run to a cab stand.

Smiling wisely, Lesal sputtered, *"Yep, this idiot is as predictable as the rest."*

Keeping a safe distance behind the cab, Lesal followed his chump to the Jersey park, then to the used car lot. Once Zane had fallen asleep at the rest area, he had done his dirty work, leaving another obvious reminder that Zane was still being trailed.

The sight of his target peeling out of the rest area in a frenzied rush had made his spine tingle with excitement. When his prey had tried to ditch him on the hi-way, Mr. Spurnell had smelled the ruse coming. He just stopped and waited in the emergency lane until he saw Zane pass him, heading south once again.

Pulling back onto the freeway in pursuit, Lesal commented jokingly, *"What a complete moron!"*

He tailed the beat-up van to a truck stop, and then waited patiently for his prey to make his next move. When Zane exited the back door wearing sunglasses and cap, Lesal saw right through the cheap disguise, chucking loudly as he watched his dupe climb into a big rig with a beastly female driver.

As he followed the pair down the freeway, Lesal knew he needed to step-up his game. It was time to start putting the fear of God into the fleeing fool, and Lesal was just the man for the job. As far as the hardnosed assassin was concerned, the real fun was just beginning.

When the rig park alongside of the road for the night, Lesal passed the pair and parked a quarter mile up the road.

Creeping up to the cab, he could hear the sounds of laughter intermixed with clinking of silverware on plates. He hid under the rig until early morning, then quietly jimmied open the cab door.

Unaware of the break in, Pat continued to snore away like a buzzsaw. Lesal pulled out a bottle of chloroform and an old handkerchief from his pocket. Soaking the rag well, he jammed it over the trucker's nose and mouth, effectively muffling her panicked gasps. Once she had conked out cold, Lesal gagged and hogtied her to the passenger seat, then tied the upper berth door with some rope. With the first part of his plan complete, he waited until sunrise.

At first light, Lesal buckled into the driver's seat and started up the engine.

Knowing that his quarry was trapped securely in the upper cabin, the hitman decided to take the big rig on a quick joy ride, just to shake things up. Revving-up the motor, he drove a quarter mile up the road, then turned sharply into a corn field.

With a high-pitched *"Yahoo!"* Lesal floored the vehicle and took it into the field, the trailer tearing apart from bouncing over the deeply furrowed rows of soil.

Positive that Zane had been rudely awakened, Lesal Spurnell brought the eighteen-wheeler to a lurching stop. Jumping out of the driver's seat in a flash, the pudgy goon swiftly waddled in the direction of his car.

Zane waited apprehensively, hiding by the truck for a good hour. As he thought over his next move, his ears caught the distinctive hum of high-speed traffic passing in the distance. Like a covey of quail flushed from the underbrush by a pointer, Zane bolted, running frantically for his life.

After reaching the interstate, Zane's fears had still not abated. He knew he had to get as far away from the area as soon as possible before the wrecked truck and Pat's bound body were discovered. Zane was terrified that the authorities would connect him to the hijacking scene and knew he would be arrested on the spot.

Standing by the side of the road, he stuck out his thumb and started hitching for a ride.

Car after car passed by, with Zane trying in earnest to look friendly and non-threatening. After several hours, he finally resigned himself to the fact that no sane motorist was going to stop to pick up a complete stranger hitch-hiking along a barren stretch of hi-way.

As Zane trudged westward, his mind was mired in a frantic blur and he felt the same feral terror of a hunted animal. His gut was churning, and his heart was racing wildly. Terrified beyond reason and unable to make a coherent decision on what to do next, Zane felt like he was swiftly going insane.

Just as he was about to lose all hope, Zane heard the toot of a car horn and the gravelly crunching of tires pulling off the road. An older gentlemen in a late model Lincoln town car opened the passenger side window and asked if he needed a ride. After giving the stranger a quick once over, Zane smiled hesitantly and hopped in.

Relieved to be safely off the roadside, he checked out the driver further.

The man seemed both friendly and harmless. He looked like a typical out-of-shape retiree, dressed in khaki shorts and faded red tee shirt. To Zane's amusement, he was sporting a well-worn Fedora and oversized goggle-style sunglasses. The tackey ensemble looked more than a bit comical, making Zane snicker inside at the geriatric drivers taste in clothing. After quick introductions, they started chatting.

"You know, I shouldn't be picking up strangers, but I get kinda' lonesome on theses long trips. It's always nice to have someone to talk to, and you seem like a nice enough guy."

Zane laughed nervously, replying, *"Thanks, you too. You never know what nutcases may be out there, just waiting to get you."*

As the driver continued to babble on, Zane's head started to nod; his mind and body absolutely exhausted from the wild yet soul chilling series of events. Feeling reassured that he was safe for the moment, he leaned his head against the window and drifted off into a restless sleep, the sound of the driver's endless jabbering slowing fading into the fuzzy darkness.

Feeling the car start to slowdown, Zane was roused from his fitful slumber.

"Sorry to wake you, but I need to stop for some gas and something to drink," the driver said apologetically. Zane nodded absently, rubbing the sleep from his eyes as he waited for his head to clear.

"Hey, would you mind doing me a favor and check the tire pressure while I'm filling up the car?" Handing Zane the gauge, the driver walked stiffly to the pump and swiped his credit card.

Zane stepped out of the car and stretched, grateful to feel his blood starved legs coming back to life. He moved to the front of the vehicle, bending over to check the pressure. While refilling a low tire, he heard the click of the pump handle and the metallic clank of the driver putting the gas nozzle back on the pump.

"Buddy, you need anything from inside?"

Zane said a bottled water would be great and headed toward the rear tires. When he moved to the rear of the car he froze in his tracks.

As plain as day was a large bumper sticker with a disgruntled face and the words, *"Have a crappy day!"* Below the scowl was a New York license plate.

Quickly looking up, he caught a glimpse of the driver as he was entering the convince store. Covering the back of his tee-shirt was a caricature of a frowning face with its tongue sticking out defiantly. The caption underneath ugly sneer read, *"Up Yours!"*

When he realized he had been riding for hours, sitting mere inches from his maniacal pursuer, Zane's mind exploded with fear.

Grabbing his bag, he ran from the car as though his very life depended on it. Screaming like a deranged banshee, he zigzagged down the road as fast as his legs could carry him. Blind with terror, Zane was almost runover by several stunned motorist, who had to slam on their brakes to avoid plowing into the berserk man.

Lesal Spurnell watched Zane's frenzied escape through the store window wearing a sadistic grin. He had not had this much fun torturing a victim in many years. Although he wanted to keep the highly entertaining drama in play indefinitely, he knew it was time to start reeling in his frantic fish.

When the clever mobster got back into his car, he pulled out a tracking devise from the glove box. While his oblivious passenger had been sleeping, Lesal had placed a small electronic tracking bug in the side pocket of the duffel bag. After turning the machine on and seeing the flashing blip on the screen, the hoodlum knew his job was going to be a breeze.

Zane fled from his stalker like a man possessed, finally collapsing to the ground when he could no longer move his aching legs another step. After a brief rest, he found a place to hide in an open garage, cowering inside a covered boat.

He waited until dusk before making his next move. Climbing from his safe haven, he jogged through the alley behind the house. Slinking about like a nervous ferret, he darted in and out of the shadows, always looking back to see if he was being followed.

The only consolation Zane felt was in the fact that he now knew the identity of his enemy.

He was now certain it was the chunky cocaine connection from New York, and Zane was convinced he was out to kill him.

He assumed the man must have discovered that the money was phony and was seeking revenge for being duped.

If not, he was sure that someone from the mob had placed a bounty on his head for passing the bogus cash and the fat fiend was looking to collect.

Zane wondered if he could bargain with the killer, perhaps offering him the rest of the uncut coke in exchange for his life. Quickly shaking the thought from his head, Zane knew without a doubt that he was a dead man. Once there was an offer of a paid hit, he was certain that nothing would deter a hired gun from collecting his fee.

The only thing he couldn't figure out was why the thug hadn't killed him in his sleep. Actually, none of the series of events leading up to this moment had made a lot of sense. Perhaps the crazed slayer wanted something more of him than his life, but Zane was clueless as to what that could possibly be.

Exhausted from the relentless hunt, Zane's mind had been pushed to the brink of madness. He felt entirely confused and disoriented, with nowhere to turn. Breaking into tears of frustration, the distraught counterfeiter picked up his bag and started walking aimlessly through the unfamiliar neighborhood, no longer sure of what he could do to evade his untimely demise.

As the sun started to set, Zane wandered into a treelined park and sat down on a bench. Drained to the core, he no longer cared what happened to him. At this point, Zane just wanted the chase to end.

"I'm here all alone you miserable bastard. Come and get me!" he screamed out frantically. *"If you're going to kill me, just get it over with."*

As the dimming sun painted the sky in foreboding dark hues, Zane lowered his head in defeat, confident that his life was going to end most tragically.

CHAPTER 3
ZANE'S AWAKENING

As he sat on the park bench, wallowing in self-pity, he failed to notice an elderly woman with a cane slowly hobbling toward him. As she carefully lowered herself to sit, the teary-eyed fugitive looked up, obviously peeved.

"My poor dear, why are you crying? What on earth could make such a handsome young man like you so upset?" she asked in a kind but croaky voice.

At the end of his rope and wanting to be left alone to face his fate, Zane blurted out, *"Keep on moving you nosey old bag. You're fouling the air with your geriatric stench."*

Completely taken aback by the ugly words, the elderly woman quickly stood up in a huff.

To his astonishment, she and began to laugh with surprising gusto, the loud chortle clearly resounding with masculine overtones. Bewildered by the unexpected humorous reaction, Zane was shocked to see the cackling old biddy take a gun out of her purse and pointing it directly at his head.

Looking about to make sure that they were alone, the old woman pulled off her grey wig and Zane gasped, recognizing his stalker instantly. Sitting back down with the gun neatly hidden under the handbag, Lesal Spurnell started to speak.

"So, we meet again, my flighty friend. First of all, you should be a bit more careful as to who you purposely insult. And, just so you know, I thought I looked damn good for an old geezer."

"Why don't you just kill me now, I can't take this crap any longer," Zane mumbled nervously.

"Be patient, my suicidal friend. We have plenty of time to chat before I need to shoot you."

After indulging in a brief chuckle over the irony of his twisted statement, Lesal became deadly serious. *"As a matter of fact, I would prefer that you to remain amongst the living for a little while longer."*

"Believe it or not, you are of much more value to me alive than dead. You're talent for making counterfeit money has not gone unnoticed. Even after counting every single bill, my boss was completely hoodwinked by your skills. You would have fooled me as well, but by chance, I caught the repeated serial numbers."

"To be honest, I've grown weary of working for the Syndicate."

"After seeing your counterfeiting expertise, I have decided to break away from my overdemanding boss and start my own business venture. With your artistry and my connections, we can make a lot of dough. All you have to do is to accompany me back to New York and do exactly what I tell you."

"Of course, if you don't agree with my proposal, I will put a bullet through your brain and take back the cocaine to sell for myself. Either way, I will profit handsomely from the deal."

Seeing no way to escape at the moment, Zane nodded in resignation and the pair slowly made their way to the town car.

Once they had settled in the vehicle, Lesal turned to Zane with a self-satisfied grin, saying, *"Yes, I think this arrangement is going to work out very well for both of us."*

With the tone of utter submission in his voice, Zane simply responded, *"I give up… I'll do whatever you want."*

After checking into a motel room for the evening, Lesal decided to test the loyalty of his new partner. Already knowing that the uncut cocaine was still in his bag, he asked Zane what he had done with the drugs.

Without hesitation, Zane opened the duffel bag. He dumped the drugs on the bed and glared at Lesal. *"Good boy"* was the goon's only comment, and he placed the coke back in Zane's satchel.

"I didn't want that crap, but I did want to see if you'd be upfront with me. As long as we're both being honest, I found eight-grand in the bottom pocket of your bag. I thought it might be safer if I locked it up in my car."

Zane was about to protest but felt like his entire world was rapidly being sucked into a bleak and endless nightmare. Not willing to push his luck with Lesal, the only thing he wanted at the moment was to crawl into his bed and sleep for a year. Without saying a word, he kicked off his shoes and pulled the covers over his head.

Just as he was about to fall into a restless slumber, he heard Lesal callout from the other side of the room, *"Goodnight, partner. Make sure to get your sleep. When we get back to the Big Apple, you're going to be working your ass off."*

Zane pulled the pillow over his head, thinking, *"Holy crap, what have I gotten myself into?"*

Early the next morning, Zane slowly crawled out of bed, still exhausted from the previous days drama. He had stayed awake most of the night with his mind churning over his maddening predicament.

If he cooperated with his captor, Zane knew he would stay alive only as long as the thug needed him. However, once he had produced the bogus bills in large enough quantities, his services would no longer be required. When that time arrived, Zane was certain that Lesal Spurnell would happily grease him and dump his corpse into the East River without a care in the world.

After putting together all the pieces of his fragile and short-lived future, the frantic counterfeiter was convinced that he had to escape from his undesirable business partner as speedily as possible.

Zane grabbed his bag and headed to the bathroom. After turning on the hot water spigot, he opened the duffel. As he searched the side pocket, looking for his tooth brush, an unexpected glint of metal caught his eye.

With some effort, he was able to pry off the mysterious object, soon realizing that the devise was some sort of tracking beacon.

"So that's how the bastard was able to find me," Zane silently mused. Stepping into the shower, he started plotting of a way to flee from his treacherous associate.

After toweling off, Zane glanced at his reflection in the mirror. To his alarm, he looked like he had aged ten years. He knew the stress of his predicament was slowly killing him, yet he still hadn't come up with a viable scheme to evade his captor.

Digging back into his bag, he pulled out a shirt and some rolled up jeans.

As he shook out his pants, Pat's gun unexpectedly fell to the floor with a deafening clank. With all the chaos of the past two days, he had completely forgotten about the weapon. He quickly retrieved the handgun, wrapping it in a pair of dirty boxers and placing it back in the bottom of the bag.

As Zane brushed his teeth; he mulled over the idea of having to kill his smarmy new business partner.

He had never fired a weapon before and wasn't sure if he had the guts to murder another man. After rinsing out his mouth in the sink, Zane decided that he would use the gun only as a last resort. If forced into the situation, he prayed he would have the fortitude to slay Lesal to save his own life. After combing his hair, Zane put the tracking device in his pocket, with an escape plan in mind.

When he entered the bedroom, Lesal was sitting on the bed watching TV. There were two white cups filled with steaming coffee sitting on the nightstand next to him.

"Hey there, my main man, I got you some java from the front office. It tastes like dirt, but it will wake you up real fast," the porky pit-bull said with a grin.

"By the way, I'm glad to see you're okay. It sounded like you tripped over a machine gun on the bathroom floor."

Zane smiled weakly, quickly heading for the coffee on the table. Grabbing the Styrofoam cup, he took a careful swig.

With fresh clothes in hand, the naked hoodlum headed for the shower. As he was about to close the door, he turned to Zane.

"Glad to see you're looking a little better. Once we're back on the road, I promise that we'll stop for some breakfast!" With a wink and a grin, the gruesome gangster walked into the bathroom singing, *"We're in the money!"*

As he strutted away, croaking painfully out of key, the sight of Lesal's gargantuan, hairy backside made his new partner gag in disgust. Luckily for Zane, the stomach-churning sight was short-lived.

He waited until he heard the repugnant goon turning on the shower, and quickly made his move. He grabbed a chair from the desk and quietly jammed it under the bathroom's doorknob.

When he discovered Mr. Spurnell's wallet sitting on the bed, he stole the cash and credit cards, stuffing them into his pocket. Wanting to get his drug money as well, he started to search Lesal's suitcase for the car keys. After searching frantically and finding nothing, he assumed that they were probably in pants the thug had carried into the bathroom.

Cursing under his breath, Zane knew he needed to flee post haste.

Running out of the hotel room, he saw a family of vacationers getting into their car. Zane gave them a friendly hello and asked the driver where they were off to.

"We're heading to Orlando. The kids have been chewing my ear off all year about going to Disney World."

Zane smiled broadly, wishing them a safe journey.

Hearing the distinctive clunk of auto's drive gear engage, he quickly ducked behind the departing vehicle, planting the tracking devise inside the rear bumper. As the Florida bound car pulled onto the highway, Zane waved goodbye, and started running frantically in the opposite direction.

CHAPTER 4
THE GETAWAY

ZANE FLAGGED DOWN THE first cab he saw, sliding into the back seat and ordering the cabbie to take him to the next closest town. As the taxi pulled into traffic, he emptied his pockets and started counting the spoils he had lifted from the hefty hoodlum. Zane smiled from ear to ear after realizing he had over three-thousand bucks in cash.

As the vehicle rolled westward, Zane replayed the getaway plan in his mind.

He assumed it would take the disgusting degenerate twenty minutes to finish showering and figure out he was locked in the bathroom. After adding another ten minutes for the troll to be able to break out of the bathroom and realize his pigeon had fled, Zane assumed he had a good half an hour of lead time. By the time Lesal dressed and got into his car to turn on the GPS tracker, Zane would be in the next town, buying a getaway vehicle.

If his luck held out, it would take the thug a few hours to catch-up with the eastbound vacationers. By the time Lesal finally caught up to the SUV and realized he had been duped, Zane would have a good four-hour head start, with Mr. Spurnell far behind him.

Having been so rattled by the events of the past few days, Zane wasn't completely sure what state he was in. He peered out the window searching for road markers. In less than a minute, he saw a sign reading, *"Leaving the town of Conway Arkansas, hope ya'll come back real soon!"*

Zane asked the cabbie where he was headed. *"We'll be in Russellville in forty minutes,"* was the reply. Inwardly amused, Zane couldn't help but smile at the town's pedestrian name. With each passing mile, he slowly started to think that he had a very good chance of getting away from the creepy con, and his mood started to rise.

The escapee had the cab driver drop him off at a used car lot. Thirty minutes later he was driving an army green Ford Taurus. Back on I-40, Zane resumed his original getaway plan and drove west.

When his stomach started to growl insistently, Zane exited the freeway at the town of Shawnee.

Driving into the small hamlet, he found a burger joint on the main drag and parked behind the building. After ordering a large number one combo, he found a table facing the street.

While wolfing down the greasy meal with gusto, Zane watched a trickle of traffic pass by the window. From what he could tell, there wasn't much going on in the backwoods, Podunk town since less than a half-dozen cars had driven by in the last twenty minutes.

While finishing off the rest of his soda, Zane's eye caught the sight of a familiar looking car driving slowly down the street, and he couldn't quite fathom what he was witnessing.

Beyond belief, it was Lesal Spurnell approaching, slowly canvassing both sides of the road. Zane quickly ducked down before the vehicle's dreaded driver passed lazily by the restaurant. Once Lesal had disappeared down the road, Zane flew to his car and peeled away, his tires screeching like Buddhist trapped in a Baptist church service.

Lesal had been somewhat surprised when he found himself locked in the bathroom. Instead of panicking and trying to knock down the door, he simply squeezed his fat carcass through the bathroom window and reentered through the front door.

With Zane nowhere to be seen, he grinned widely, knowing that the chase was back on. When he saw his emptied wallet, Lesal had to give his reluctant business partner some credit for careful planning.

"It's about time that brainless dope started thinking ahead."

From the phone in the motel office, the gangster called his boss, requesting additional time off.

"Take all the time you need," was Axel's immediate response.

Tickled at the thought that the pudgy goon was going to be out of his hair for a few more weeks, the mob chief patted himself on the back for his quick thinking and poured out a tumbler of scotch in celebration.

After checking on Zane's cash in the glove box, Lesal turned on his GPS locater. Scrutinizing the blip on the screen, he scratched his head in disbelief. From what he could tell, his runaway was traveling eastbound at seventy miles-per-hour.

Unfortunately for Zane, no one could smell a con like conman, and Lesal wasn't buying the info the tracker was telling him.

"Why would the idiot be traveling back east? Doesn't he know that he would be heading back toward certain trouble," the savvy criminal pondered. *"No, if Zane had originally fled to the west, that would be the same direction he'd want to continue going.*

"Stupid humans are always creatures of habit," the gangster muttered under his breath.

Well aware that his unenthusiastic partner had finally put some preemptive scheming into his escape, Lesal took a chance and assumed that Zane had found the tracking devise. More than likely, he had purposely planted it on a vehicle going in the opposite direction as a decoy. *"Smart move, Mr. Worth"* he thought, *"but not smart enough."*

Confident that his prey would be stubbornly following the direction of the sun, so was Lesal.

After seeing the town of Russellville on the map, Lesal had a gut feeling and set a direct course for the small rural community.

After recalling Zane past escape attempts, he had either hitched a ride, or hailed a cab. Either way, he was sure that his chump would want his own transportation, and with Lesal's stolen cash, he would most likely go for another cheap used car.

At the used car lot in Russellville, he questioned the salesman to see if anyone had dropped in.

"Yep, had one sale so far today, to a city slicker with blue eyes, black hair, and lots of cash. Not the smartest feller though. Bought a puke green, piece-o-crap rust bucket, then drove away happier than a pimp in a Porsche."

When he asked the salesman which way the buyer had gone, the old codger laughed, replying, *"Took off like a bat outta hell, headin' west on 40."* Lesal gave him a twenty for the info and got back on the interstate.

As he approached Shawnee, he had another hunch. Knowing that Zane hadn't eaten in quite a while, he'd probably stop somewhere off the beaten path to catch a quick bite on the run. As he cruised down the main drag, he had passed several fast-food joints, but had not spotted his mark. Hungry himself, he stopped at taco stand to order lunch.

While chowing down on his belly busting fare, Lesal was grinning from ear to ear.

The hunt was back on, and his prey had the advantage of knowing much more about him than before. To Lesal, this was life at its very best, and he knew he had all the time in the world to find his valuable counterfeiter.

He was confident that sooner or later, he would recapture Zane and this time he would take no chance on losing him again. That scenario would have proven its self highly unprofessional to a consummate pro like Lesal Spurnell.

CHAPTER 5
FROM THE FRYING PAN,
INTO THE FIRE

ZANE FLEW DOWN THE freeway like Cerberus was snapping at his heels.

He was shocked that Lesal had seen through his rouse so easily and had caught up with him in less than an hour. He wondered if the man had supernatural powers and felt like he was never going to evade the stumpy, tenacious tracker.

As he questioned over how quickly Lesal had caught up with him, Zane realized his actions had been far too predictable.

"He knew I was heading west, and I have never veered from that direction," he reasoned angrily. *"I've been a complete fool and have vastly underestimated this monster's underworld expertise."*

By the time he had reached the outskirts of Oklahoma City, Zane had initiated a new plan. To throw off his bloated bloodhound, he knew he needed to change direction, so he took the I-35 south ramp. To permanently evade the diabolical tracker, he needed to get hold of a lot more money.

His knew his plan was dicey, but he needed to steal enough cash to get to Fort Worth, then quickly catch a jet to anywhere out of the country.

When he reached the small town of Norman, he stopped at a small bank branch. He put on his baseball cap and sunglasses, then shoved Pat's gun it into his waistband. He had selected the small financial institution off the main thoroughfare, hoping that the clueless rubes would be unprepared for a robbery.

As he entered the bank building, there was an ancient looking security guard, napping soundly in an overstuffed armchair by the water cooler. Definitely pleased with his decision, Zane walked up casually to the one and only teller with a friendly grin.

"Good afternoon and welcome to Norman Savings and Loan," the overly cheerful blonde chirped in a thick southern drawl. *"And how can I help you today?"*

"Well, let me see" Zane mocked sarcastically, mildly amused at her small-town naiveté. Imitating her phony-baloney demeanor, he sang out sweetly, *"I would like to make a modest withdrawal, say a paltry twenty-thousand dollars."*

"Absolutely," the teller twittered back perkily. *"May I please have your account number?"*

Zane pulled the gun from his pants and pointed it at her head, growling contemptuously, *"Here's my fricken account number, you brainless bimbo!"*

The ditzy teller became so verklempt, she started to faint. Zane had to reach inside her cubbyhole and grab her by the collar, or the highly distraught woman would have collapsed to the floor.

As Zane struggled to keep the teller standing upright, he failed to notice a small elderly woman entering the bank. She slowly took her place in line and opened her purse. Taking out her passbook with hushed reverence, she started flipping fondly through its many pages.

Mrs. Buswell had been a customer of the establishment for most of her life. At the tender age of ten, her father had helped her open a savings account and she had been depositing her nest egg money into it for the past seventy years.

As she watched the strange man struggling with the bank clerk, Mrs. Buswell became alarmed. When she could no longer quell her curiosity, the frail looking great grandmother leaned forward, tapping Zane urgently on the shoulder.

"Young man, what are you doing to that teller?" she queried insistently.

At that point Zane had endured far too many distractions. He spun around and screamed at the nosey old crow, *"I'm trying to rob this asinine bank, so please shut the hell up and mind your own business!"*

He turned back to the traumatized teller, now extremely irritated by the absurd situation. Slowly snapping out of her stupor, the woman started screeching for help at the top of her lungs.

Putting his gun to her head, Zane warned, *"I have a mind to shoot you between the eyes, but I don't think the bullet would damage anything of importance. If I were you, I would stop screaming and give me all your money before I have to prove my point."*

When the bank clerk finally managed to open the cash drawer, Zane quickly cased the room one last time. The pathetic guard was still sleeping, his snores clearly audible over the mind-numbing country music being piped into the building.

With no one else around, beside the snoopy old bag behind him, he started waving his gun threateningly at the clerk, telling her to speed it up and bag the cash. Regrettably, he failed to notice sweet Mrs. Buswell rummaging through her purse and pulling out a pearl handled derringer.

As he reached forward to grab the loot from the brainless teller, he heard a sharp pop, and his left buttock instantly felt like it was on fire.

Falling to the floor in excruciating pain, he looked up in a daze to see the livid octogenarian glaring down at him, swinging her oversized purse. She bludgeoned the downed bank robber repeatedly with all her might, screaming, *"How dare you try to steal my hard-earned money. You're a terrible man and you must be punished!"*

All the ruckus finally roused the guard from his midday siesta. He stood up unsteadily, then started fumbling for his pistol.

Noticing that the bank's pitiful protector was finally awake, Mrs. Buswell screamed, *"Bank Robber! Clyde, you old fool, shoot that filthy bandit!"* Stunned by the chaos, and blind as a bat, Clyde was so flustered that he started firing shots randomly at anything that moved.

When the smoke slowly cleared, the dizzy blonde teller and poor Mrs. Buswell were on the floor, soaked in pools of their own blood. Zane was also on the floor with his arms over his head, cowering in fear.

Slowly realizing that the bank robber was the only person still alive, Clyde started digging around franticly in his pants pocket, searching for more bullets. Luckily for Zane, the police arrived just as the dementia prone guard had reloaded his weapon.

When he saw the officers rushing in, Zane screamed out hysterically, *"Thank God you're here. Arrest me and drag me to prison! Whatever you do, put it in gear and get me the hell out of this den of insanity!"*

When Lesal Spurnell awoke the next morning, he turned on the TV to catch up on world events.

Just as he was about to step into the shower, his ear caught a breaking news story of a robbery in the small municipality of Norman. Walking back into the bedroom, he was bowled over to watch a video clip of Zane Worth being dragged from the credit union, kicking and screaming hysterically.

The reporter went on to say that two local people had been mortality injured in the botched robbery attempt, and that perpetrator had been locked up in the county jail without bail.

Next up, was a dim-witted old guard trying to recall the events of the crime. After listening to more than enough of the old geezer's mindless rambling, Lesal angrily drew his Glock 9mm from his leg holster and shot a hole through the TV screen.

The hitman was beside himself with rage. Cursing and fuming, he walked into the shower and turned on the cold-water tap. After standing in the icy spray for a half-hour, he had finally cooled down enough to think clearly.

While packing his bags for the journey back to New York, a droll grin formed on Lesal's lips. This was the first time in his lengthy criminal career that he had failed to capture his mark, yet he realized that all was not lost. Sooner or later, he was certain that Zane would be released. On that fateful day, he would be waiting impatiently at the front gate of the penitentiary to meet him.

Until that time arrived, he would wait to see where they incarcerated his cagey counterfeiter and make a few calls. Lesal knew more than a few fellow mobsters locked away in prisons around the country and would arrange to have his chump protected from the rest of the unpredictable inmates.

Still shaking his head in disbelief, the humiliated hoodlum hopped into his Lincoln and started his three-day trek back to the east coast.

CHAPTER 6
ZANE SINGS THE PRISON BLUES

AFTER THE BRIEFEST TRIAL in the history of the Sooner State, Zane was sentenced to twenty-five years for attempted robbery.

With time off for good behavior, he hoped he would be released in eight to ten, not that the thought gave him any real comfort. As he stepped into the prison transport bus bound for the Oklahoma State Penitentiary, Zane was enveloped in a fog of depression.

To his consternation, Zane's court appointed public defender had been a passionate born-again Christian. He had insisted that Zane plead guilty to avoid being damned to Hell for eternity. Zane had begrudgingly agreed, hopeful that his open and honest admission of guilt might provoke some leniency from the court.

When the judge heard Zane's admission of guilt, he cracked a cruel smirk.

Slamming down his gavel with great bravura, he ordered the maximum sentence allowable by law. Staring down at the condemned bank robber with a look of utter contempt, he lectured piously, *"You are a boil on the face of society, repulsive and morally festered. I would advise that you use your time in prison to change your dastardly ways and seek redemption in the eyes of our Lord."*

With a glare of unmitigated hatred, he added, *"If I ever see you in my courtroom again, I will fry your ass like a pork chop in a red-hot skillet."*

⋙❊⋘

As the ancient prison transport rumbled down the interstate, Zane looked absently out the window, trying to prepare his mind for the lengthy incarceration.

He realized glumly that he would be sharing the next two decades of his life with rapists, murders, and the worst scum of society. The very though made him shudder with trepidation, and he felt a horrific sinking feeling in the pit his stomach.

He silently kicked himself for not submitting to Lesal Spurnell and his plans. At least, in that case, he would have had a chance to escape if he felt his life was in imminent danger.

Staring blankly out the window, his eye caught a sign down the road and he read the billboard's message with some mild annoyance.

"Jesus Saves," was all the sanctimonious bill board said. In a fleeting moment of mirth, Zane's eyes narrowed, and he mumbled, *"But God invests."*

Softly chuckling at his joke in self-pity, he looked about the bus at his fellow prisoners. They all were facing forward in silence, some of the convicted felons almost in tears. Curious as to who was sitting behind him, he turn his gaze to the back of the bus. As his eyes rested on a huge, tattoo covered man with a badly healed scar across his chin; the behemoth inmate gave him a prolonged wink and licked his lips lasciviously.

Quickly turning back around with an involuntary shudder, Zane decided it might be best to just keep his eyes looking forward.

As he absently looked back out the window at an overly large bill board, he could not believe his eyes.

Staring back at him was a huge unhappy face with the message, *"Have a crappy couple of decades, Mr. Worth,"* followed by, *"See you when you get out!"*

Already on edge of a nervous breakdown, Lesal's cruel message made him instantly nauseous and he retched violently over the inmate in front of him.

Turning around with a glare of unmitigated hate, the puke-soaked con started punching Zane's face brutally. Luckily for Mr. Worth, by that point he was far too numb to feel a thing.

Other than losing his privacy, dignity, and his last shred of self-esteem, Zane found the slammer somewhat bearable.

He quickly discovered if he masked his insecurities with a continual scowl, most of the inmates left him alone. *"Prison really isn't half as bad as everyone said,"* he mused.

In actuality, if it had not been for Mr. Spurnell's arrangements to keep him protected, Zane would have soon succumbed to the varied and perverse whims of each and every convict. Being a vulnerable and eye-catching young man was definitely not an advantage when you were locked up behind bars.

His cell mate, nicknamed Slim, was a fellow bank robber and they seemed to bond immediately. Slim mentored Zane on the rules of prison life, which were exceedingly simple and straightforward. The first and foremost rule was to protect your back. The only way to accomplish that lifesaving necessity was to join the appropriate gang.

By the end of the first week, Zane had become a fully-fledged member of the white supremacists.

As part of the skinhead's obligatory ritual, they shaved him bald and started patterning future gang identification tattoos on his chest and arms with a magic marker. Petrified with fear, Zane was utterly helpless to deter the situation.

If matters couldn't get any worse, the perverse gang leader took a liking to him and made the newbie a mascot of sorts. When out of his cell, Zane had to wear a spiked dog collar and his master, known as *Chaos,* proudly paraded him around the grounds on a leash like a pedigreed pooch.

Although the situation was extremely degrading, *Fifi* was now safe from the malevolent antics of the rest of prison population.

No matter what indignities the inmate had to endure, Zane kept his eyes fixated on the clock, waiting impatiently for 8PM to finally roll around. That's when dinner and free time was over. A few hours later, it was lights-out for the night. Once back in his cell, *Fifi* would rip off his collar and try to shake off the shame of being dragged around the prison by *Chaos.*

Slim tried to give his cellmate some much-needed reassurance, but Zane soon fell into a deep depression.

The new convicts life had become a nightmarish routine. After rising up at 6AM, then taking a quick shower and pulling on his orange jumpsuit, Zane would head for the dining area. After shoving down the tasteless swill, he would slowly shuffle to the outside yard where his master would be waiting with his leash in hand.

Day after day, week after week, and month after month, Zane re-lived the same demeaning scenario, gradually growing to despise his shameful existence.

One early morning, *Fifi* abruptly awoke, barking and howling like a junk yard dog at the top of his lungs.

Slim had to slap him soundly across the face several times to get him to pipe down. When Zane had regained a smidgen his fragile sanity, he made a life affirming decision. In his tortured mind, he knew he had to get *Chaos* out of the picture and had devised an underhanded plan to rid himself of his debasing master.

While waiting in the grub line, Zane asked one of the servers if there was a spot in the kitchen. When he was informed of an opening, Zane quickly wrote the warden to apply.

After having his job confirmed by the prison's work administrator, he was placed in a food servers position and Zane was thrilled. He now had three shifts a day doling out grub to the inmates, and for the work, he was to be paid twenty-five cents an hour.

The best part of the deal was that he would now be away from his despised handler for most of the day, thus regaining a fragment of his shattered self-worth.

When *Chaos* heard of Zane's unexpected job appointment he became highly enraged. However, as the leader of the skinheads mulled over the situation he slowly calmed down, knowing that he could now get *Fifi* to give him double portions of food at each meal. It seemed like a fair tradeoff since *Chaos* had grown tired of his moody and unappreciative pup.

Unfortunately, the fickle finger of fate poked Slim with a vengeance when the gang leader discovered that he had given Zane the food server tip. Seeking revenge for the loss of his pretty pooch, *Chaos* appointed him to be the new gang bitch.

Not only did Slim have to wear the accursed collar, but *Chaos* painted his toe and finger nails bright pink. To top-off the foo-foo couture, poor *Fifi 2* had to wear a pink bow with fake floppy dog ears taped to his shaved head.

When Zane had earned enough cash, he sought out the one con who had access to all the illicit products banned by the prison staff.

From chewing gum to heroin, *Lumpy* was the go-to guy. He had earned his nickname from the mass of badly healed bumps on his head from being pummeled mercilessly by the guard's riot sticks.

Lumpy had earned a sterling reputation for not only being able to find most anything for his incarcerated customers, but for keeping all of his illicit dealings highly secretive.

When Zane asked him what drugs were available, Lumpy started going down his extensive list of products. Not hearing the name of what he was looking for, Zane asked if he could get some Coumadin. Since the con wasn't the least bit familiar with the drug Zane had requested, Lumpy said to come back in a week.

Zane's vengeful plan was ingeniously simple. Well aware that drug he sought was a powerful blood thinner, he planned to crush up ten times the normal dosage and surreptitiously add it to his despised leader's daily rations. Before every meal he would mix the drug in the corner of one of his food pan. When it was time to dish out his master's portion, he would scoop out the tainted food from the appropriate area with a genial smile. He was certain, that in no time, *Chaos* would be sick as a dog himself.

Three weeks later, in the middle of dinner, *Chaos* collapsed face down into his metal tray. When the guards pulled his mug out of a mound of Macaroni and Cheese, the con was bleeding profusely out of his mouth, nose, and ears. By the time the leader of the skinheads had reached the infirmary, he had already expired from massive internal hemorrhaging.

After lights out, Zane confessed to his cellmate. He told Slim that he had only wanted his despised master to become intensely ill, but certainly not to die. He felt horrible about the situation, and hoped his gang was not going to seek reprisals for their leader's unintended demise.

Upon hearing the news, Slim was so overjoyed that he ran to Zane and gave him a bear hug so hard that he almost cracked his cell mates ribs.

After calming down, Slim swore his undying loyalty to Zane, and said that he would happily obey any command his best friend might request. Zane laughed heartily, then apologized to his bunkmate for having to take over his mascot duties. He said that all he really required was to have his friend watch his back, and Slim gratefully accepted the task. Zane also insisted that his pal keep the poisoning a secret from the rest of the gang.

Being a bit weak of character, Slim was unable to keep his fat trap shut.

By the end of the following morning's breakfast period, the entire prison was abuzz with the shocking news that submissive little *Fifi* was the daring con that had cunningly off'd *Chaos*.

When he met up with his gang, Zane was met with stone cold silence. Immediately growing anxious by the icy reception, Zane's worries were soon eased.

Slim spoke for the group, informing him that the boys were so impressed with his unabashed bravery, that they had unanimously voted him in as the new leader of the gang.

Knowing that it would be foolhardy to ignore his fellow skinheads wishes, Zane reluctantly agreed to his dubious promotion.

Every so often, violent power struggles would break out between the rival gangs.

In an effort to establish some peace and tranquility, Zane convinced the other gang leaders into adopting a mutual truce. He argued that if they all could work together; they would be a united and unstoppable force.

With Zane as their appointed leader, the entire inmate population started to alter their overtly aggressive behaviors. Over a short period of time, civility started to reign throughout the penitentiary.

With the inmate's behavior becoming far less berserk, Zane called a meeting with the guards and the offer was straightforward. If they helped him get the various supplies the prisoners wanted; they would no longer have to worry about their safety.

At first, the guards rejected the idea outright, knowing that convicted felons were not typically men of their word. As prison life remained calm and peaceful, the guards slowly relented and started a secret trade agreement with Zane.

Any reasonable items that were requested by the inmates, the guards started smuggling in. In return, the officers were rewarded with ten- percent of the profits. As long as the convicts were able to hide their contraband from the warden, the surreptitious business arrangement would continue.

Never in his wildest dreams did Zane think he would rule over the entire prison population.

Luckily, the ideas he initiated had worked like a charm and order and harmony ruled the day. The incarcerated men were unusually contented, and the guards were extremely happy with their secure work environment.

For his efforts, Zane now had more luxuries in prison that he had ever possessed on the outside. From a plasma TV and internet cable in his cell, to catered food flown in from the best restaurants in New York City, Zane Worth was living high on the hog.

One evening during a gathering of the gang leaders, the subject of a breakout was presented for debate.

The leader of the Hispanic group believed, with the guards being so lax, that a breakout would be a piece of cake. Zane, who was perfectly contented to remain safe on the inside and far away from Mr. Spurnell's diabolical grasp, argued vehemently against the idea. After an hour of heated debate, Zane assumed that he had finally quashed the idea for good.

Unbeknownst to the boss of the skinheads, the other gang leaders had conducted a few more series of clandestine meetings with the rest of the inmates. The final consensus of the cabal was to formulate a breakout plan without Zane being aware of the scheme.

When Lumpy was ordered to smuggle in plastic explosives, he choked, saying that even the most brain-dead guard would refuse to cooperate. When the contraband specialist was given no choice in the matter, he hesitantly agreed, informing the gang bosses that it would take some time to make all the arrangements.

A few months later, as the guards performed their obligatory checks on the supplies shipped into the prison; they were amused to see four cases of Play-Doh along with the usual crates of cigarettes, booze, and pot.

One of the officers opened up a tub and took out the green colored paste, molding it into a fake gun. Pointing the roughhewn weapon at his buddy, he joked sarcastically, *"Hands up, sucker!"*

Completely unaware that the substance was actually C-4, the clueless guard packed the explosive back into its container, commenting, *"Jeez, those goofy felons are turning into a bunch of children."*

On the evening of the breakout, the inmates had planned a major party event for the penitentiary staff.

The ruse was presented as a celebratory dinner to honor a new era of cooperation between the guards and their prisoners.

The convicts spared no expense, buying lobster, prime rib, and champagne to commemorate the new peace accord. As planned, the penitentiary staff were entirely unaware that the food had been laced with a potent tranquilizer strong enough to drop an elephant. To keep the bust out a secret from the big boss, Zane was left completely in the dark.

Astonished by the news of the unexpected banquet, Zane gave Slim a slightly distrustful look as he walked into the mess hall. To his amazement, the inmates were pouring glasses of Dom Perignon to the guards, while other prisoners were bringing out heaping platters of high-class fare.

As the security staff started to dig into the feast, their hosts stuck to drinking and toasting to their captors. Clueless and going with the flow, Zane sat down and started to gorge down on the fancy fixings along with the guards.

To his credit, Lumpy had done his homework impeccably.

Along with obtaining the C-4, he had had secured blueprints of the prison and the surrounding infrastructure. The schematics showed a six-foot drainage pipe directly below the basement laundry facility that connected to the main sewer system leading into town.

Slim's task had been to formulate a distraction to throw off the police. It had to be dramatic enough to give the escaping prisoners adequate lead time. He knew that if they had blown through the outer walls to escape, it wouldn't take long for the local authorities to hear the explosions and quickly intervene.

Instead, he packed a small charge with just enough explosive to blast through the basement floor leading to the escape pipe. The rest of the C-4 was attached to the main prison entrance and set to detonate when the doors were opened from the outside.

Thirty minutes into the dinner, all the guards and Zane Worth were completely comatose from the tainted fare.

With the guards' prison keys in hand, the inmates planted the explosives and then returned to the cafeteria. With military precision, the men made their way down to the basement with a change of civilian clothes in hand. Still out like a light, Slim threw Zane over his shoulder. With a heavy sigh, he started to lug his slumbering boss down to the basement.

The detonation inside the laundry facility was louder than expected, but Lumpy was sure that the handful of guards patrolling the outside perimeter of the building would not hear a thing. Knowing that a fresh crew of security personnel would be arriving within the hour, the entourage of four hundred convicts filed into the pipe heading to the sewer main.

With Lumpy leading the way, the prisoners slogged through a quarter mile of human dreck and climbed out of a manhole behind a local gas station.

The convicts quickly changed clothes and headed out on their own. Finally, a very red-faced Slim appeared, sweat soaked and completely exhausted from dragging Zane's dead weight through the sewer. After changing out Zane's prison garb, and their own clothing, Lumpy and Slim grabbed their pal under his arms, lugging him to a nondescript Dodge van that Lumpy had arranged to be waiting for them.

Chucking Zane in the back, the two cons jumped into the vehicle and sped south.

Right on schedule, the midnight shift of guards met at the gate and made their way to the front entrance. When the doors were opened, there was an enormous blast, with many misfortunate men thrown several hundred feet into the air. The explosions instantly set off the alarms and absolute mayhem broke out.

The warden arrived twenty minutes later, accompanied by hundreds of police officers and several dozen FBI agents at his side. He was momentarily shaken at the sight of his men's bodies littering the entry way. Upon entering the building, he was even more stunned by the absolute silence. There were simply no guards or inmates to be seen.

When the entourage of law enforcement officers entered the cafeteria, the warden was completely flabbergasted. Still snoozing away were his entire day staff, covered in confetti and wearing children's silly party hats. Empty champagne bottles were strewn everywhere, with platters of half-eaten lobster and beef covering the tables.

Normally an unflappable individual who could handle any situation professionally, the warden instantly collapsed to his knees and started crying like a baby. The FBI chief quickly got on his walkie talkie, calling in an astonishing APB on four hundred escaped convicts.

Lesal Spurnell was perched on the trunk of his car, gazing down at the sprawling metropolis of Las Vegas below. It was well past 2 AM, and the blazing neon lights of the strip filled the valley below with the harsh glare of false hopes and shattered dreams.

His mark was in front of him, digging into the rocky desert earth with bare hands, his labored breathing the only sound marring the quiet hush of the evening.

When the hole was sufficiently deep, Lesal barked at the man to jump inside and lay face down. The terrified pigeon pleaded with him for mercy, his panic induced blathering only pissing-off the grouchy goon. With one precise shot to the back of the head, the desert ridge was once more, silent and peacefully serene.

Not bothering to coverup his misdeed, the gangster assumed that the first good rain would fill the hole with gravelly mud. If not, he was certain the coyotes and buzzards would make quick work of the cadaver. Either way, his work here was done.

As Lesal got back into his car the assassin let out a resigned sigh. In his tormented mind, he had become entirely disenchanted with his career. His bosses never-ending commands echoed relentlessly through his skull.

"Slit that bastard's throat. Torture that skinflint and bring me back his severed finger. Bash-in that deadbeat's skull. Kill... kill... kill!" all looped endlessly through his spent brain.

Over the passing decades, Lesal had grown completely

uninspired and felt his life had become dully predictable and irrelevant. His existence held no flavor and his work had become grinding drudgery.

As he obsessed over his unctuous vocation, he became increasingly fatalistic. Lesal Spurnell had endured more than enough of his skewed life and was prepared to end his miserable and contemptible existence. With the car radio murmuring softly in the background, the mobster took his gun off the passenger seat and put it up to his head.

The reality of death didn't frighten Lesal in the least.

He had witnessed countless victims die before his eyes. Death's onslaught was always the same: a sudden look of shock, followed by a few gasping breaths, and then nothing. To be certain, he had never seen a spirit rising from the corpse to be greeted by heavenly apparitions from above, nor the clutching claws of the devil dragging the soul to endless damnation below. As far as Lesal could tell, death was simply eternal sleep.

Thinking back, he realized that he had blown a perfectly good chance to escape his sordid career.

His golden ticket to financial independence was locked away for decades, with his invaluable counterfeiting talents completely wasted. In Lesal's despondent mind, he knew he couldn't wait another twenty years to start a new profession. As far as he was concerned, it was time to check out permanently.

As he slowly started to squeeze the trigger, his ear caught an odd bit of news.

Hesitating for a moment, he turned up the radio and listened intently. To his amazement, the announcer was reporting on a breaking news story about a massive convict breakout from the state prison in McAlester, Oklahoma.

It took Lesal a few moments to process the information, and he slowly lower the revolver.

When the suicidal goon realized that each and every one of the four hundred prisoners had escaped, he shouted with uncontained glee, *"Well I'll be a son of a bitch! I can't believe that bastard's luck,"* quickly followed by, *"Thank you God, for giving me a reason to live."*

CHAPTER 7
MEXICO MADNESS

THE DAY AFTER THE breakout, Zane was roused from his drug induced stupor by the intermittent joggling of the van.

As his pupils slowly adjusted to the harsh glare of intense sunlight, he looked out the window in bewilderment. Seeing nothing but scrub covered hills and a few Saguaro cacti, he was left speechless. The last thing he had remembered was chugging Champagne and wolfing down prime rib with the prison guards in the cafeteria.

When he peered over the back seat of the van, he witnessed Lumpy driving with Slim riding shotgun. They were both wearing gaudy sombreros and guzzling downing bottles of Corona. Befuddled by the weird vision, Zane was now convinced he had finally gone totally bonkers.

When he groaned loudly, Slim looked back, commenting, *"I told ya' buddy, he's not dead. See for yourself!"* Lumpy glanced into the rear-view mirror and smiled widely. *"Morning boss, glad to see you're back amongst the living."*

Rubbing his throbbing head, all the gang leader could croak out was, *"What in hell happened last night?"*

Zane listened in awe, as Lumpy and Slim recapped the past evening's events. When the story had ended, Zane had one question. *"Where in blazes are we?"*

Lumpy looked back, shouting excitedly, *"We're in Mexico, boss... on our way to Puerto Vallarta."*

As the van slowly snaked its way south, Zane felt increasing waves of nausea wash over his body.

Part of his gastric turmoil had been induced by the excessive amount of horse tranquilizer that Lumpy had dumped into the food, now intensified tenfold by the abysmal Mexican roads.

However, the main source of his all-consuming queasiness came from the realization that he was no longer safely protected within the confines of the penitentiary walls. Back on the outside, he knew Lesal Spurnell would be actively pursuing him, and the thought filled him with reborn dread.

Having the feeling that sometime was wrong, Slim turned to Zane and questioned, *"Hey Boss, what's up? You're awfully quite back there."*

No longer able to quell his nausea or annoyance, Zane screamed for Lumpy to stop the van. Slinging open the side door, he was able to run a few steps before heaving-up the contents of his stomach. Between the waves of retching, Zane cursed at the cons, telling them in no uncertain terms what a pack of jackasses they were. When Zane had finally finished purging, he looked-up with an angry glare at his befuddled associates.

Climbing into the back seat of the van, Zane barked gruffly, *"Okay, you two numbskulls, let's get out of this fricking inferno. I already feel like I've died and gone to hell."*

As they crept their way toward the town of Guadalajara, Zane filled in his friends about Lesal Spurnell and his quest to capture him.

Once secured in his clutches, Lesal had made it clear that he planned to force his prisoner to use his phony money producing skills. Zane relayed his overwhelming fear that when Mr. Spurnell had laundered enough of the bogus cash, he would be killed by his crazed captor.

As the men sat in silence, Zane explained the sticky situation he was now dealing with.

"Once that crazy bastard hears I'm out of the pen, he will be back on my trail like a fly to manure." All Lumpy could say was, *"Sorry boss, we had no idea of what you'd be facing back on the outside."* Now aware of Zane's precarious situation, Slim chimed in, *"Don't worry pal, me and Lumpy will make sure that nothing happens to you."* Zane grimaced, responding, *"You two have no idea of what Lesal Spurnell is capable of. You both had better start growing eyes out of the back of your heads if you know what's good for you."*

With his mind finally out of its fog, Zane started wondering if the state police or FBI would be chasing him as well. If not, he was positive Lesal would be just days behind him. The mere thought made his guts twist angrily.

As the trio headed to the southern Pacific coast, Zane questioned the pair as to how they were all going to survive on the lamb. Slim grinned from ear to ear and crawled to the backseat of the van. After digging around in a canvas bag, he handed his pal a large brief case. Opening the latches, Zane was bowled over by the amount of cash inside.

"That's one-hundred grand," Slim said in hushed reverence. Lumpy chimed in, bragging, *"Your prison trade scheme work like a charm. Even after the guards cut, we were pulling in over ten thousand a month."*

As Zane gazed at the money with his jaw agape, Slim took out some documents from the top pocket of the case. He handed Zane a small red book, and then started laughing hysterically. Confused by the words *Pasaporte España* embossed on the front, Zane opened the document and started reading the contents inside.

To his amazement, there was his picture, and under it, the name Franco Maximilian. Entirely bewildered, all Zane could blurt out was, *"What the hell is this all about?"*

Slim confessed that when they had been firming up plans to breakout, Lumpy had snagged Zane's mug shot from the prison files. Realizing that they all would need some kind of valid identification, Lumpy had sent their pictures to an ex-con on the outside, infamous for producing near perfect fake passports.

"Without a doubt, they look better than the real McCoy," Slim boasted.

"Who in hell came up with the name Franco Maximilian?" Zane queried.

"That was my idea," Lumpy confessed. *"It just sounded classy and important, and Maximilian was the name of my pet Golden retriever."*

When Lumpy had finished his explanation, there was an uncomfortable period of dead silence.

After reminiscing over his "dog days" in prison as *Fifi*, Zane started snickering uncontrollably. When his cohorts realized that Zane wasn't peeved, they join in the hilarity.

With Lumpy navigating his way through the pothole-ridden highway, the three men guzzled down beers and laughing until their sides hurt. Five days later, and extremely hung-over, the escaped convicts reached their final destination.

Nestled on the Pacific Coast, the city of Puerto Vallarta was one of Mexico's few shining jewels.

The old part of town had a many quaint buildings reminiscent of the architecture of Old Spain. To Zane's surprise, the remainder of the city was comprised of thousands of new condos and Hotels catering to American and European tourists.

As the men drove through the varied neighborhoods, they noticed that the air was either filled with the heavenly scent of tropical flowers, or the heady bouquet of open sewer pipes depending on where you happened to be. When Lumpy commented on the nose confusing disparity, Zane laughed, responding," After *seven days on the road without any of us bathing, I wouldn't complain about the air outside!*"

With Margaritas in hand, the trio strolled-down the main artery of the port city. They watched in amusement, as the throngs of tourists from the cruise ships scurried about purchasing their worthless treasures. Zane was amazed at the copious piles of junk for sale in the shops, and openly questioned as to why anyone in their right mind would spend a nickel on any of the useless knickknacks.

With sarcastic chuckles all around, they walked to the beach to check out the local scenery.

All three men were amazed to see so many light skinned bathers sunning on the sands. Other than the ubiquitous throngs of Mexican children who were selling pretty much anything you could spear on a stick; you would have sworn you were in the heart of South Beach.

Zane felt reassured, knowing that blending in with the foreign tourists would be an advantage, especially since he was being hunted by Lesal Spurnell. He had been thinking about his adversary incessantly and knew he had to remain ever vigilant to avoid being discovered by the maniacal mobster.

Walking into a touristy Palapa stuffed with beach wear, Zane emerged five minutes later dressed in his new beach camouflage. Wearing flip-flops, flowery board shorts, and a tank top, Zane smiled weakly, knowing how silly he looked. His buddies were beside themselves, pointing at his tacky garb and mocking him mercilessly.

"I don't give a crap what you guys think," Zane retorted. *"At least I am blending in with the local color."*

Not wanting to be outdone, the other two felons were soon dressed in similar attire. To complete the carefree vacation look, Slim had insisted on putting straw hats atop their heads.

Dressed in their new disguises, they toasted to their new life with frosty bottles of Dos Equis. Without a care in the world, the three colorful amigos strolled leisurely down the beach.

At the far end of the sand, they came upon an older hotel with twenty or so blue wooden lounge chairs out front.

As Lumpy casually surveyed the scene, something struck him as odd. He was stunned to see that most of the patrons out sunning themselves were guys, wearing very skimpy swim wear. After further careful observations, he quickly motioned to Zane and Slim.

Once they were huddled, Lumpy whispered, *"We need to get out of here fast. I think all the dudes on the blue chairs are gay!"* As the men canvassed the beach area intently, Slim agreed.

With a plan starting to brew in his head, Zane smiled shrewdly.

"If you guys are right, this place should be perfect for our plans. I'm going to check it out right now."

As Slim and Lumpy watched in horror, Zane walked directly into the throng of scantily clad men and started asking questions. Ten minutes later, he returned to his stunned pals, stating that he had just rented three rooms at the Hotel for the next six months.

Slim was the first to stutter out, *"Have you gone insane?"* Lumpy quickly nodded in agreement, far too tongue-tied to utter a single word.

Zane explained excitedly, *"Guys, this is the ideal place to hide out. I don't think anyone would ever think to look for three escaped convicts in a gay resort."*

When the two men remained silent, Zane pleaded, *"Come on now, the guys are harmless. Like us, they are eager to enjoy their vacations and have a good time."* Lumpy finally managed to speak, mumbling nervously, *"That exactly what I'm afraid of!"*

After securing their cash in the hotel's vault, the trio walked back to the center of town looking for a place to eat.

They stumbled across a brightly painted open-air restaurant specializing in fresh sea food and chose a table on the bay side veranda. After greedily ordering one of every dish on the menu, they requested a bottle of Patron and three large glasses.

As the men dug enthusiastically into their ocean-born feast, they discussed their future plans. Zane figured that if they were somewhat prudent with the money, they could hide- out indefinitely. With Mexican prices extremely low, all they would have to do is invest the balance of the cash, and the interest on the account would easily pay the bills.

Lumpy and Slim reluctantly admitted that they were fine with the idea for the time being, and both agreed that it was about time they all had a taste of the good life. Zane concurred, now in high spirits since he felt secure and concealed in his new surroundings.

With a concerned look, Lumpy raised his hand timidly and

asked, *"Are we really going to stay at the Blue Chairs Hotel for the next six months?"*

Zane and Slim glanced at each other and immediately started chuckling. After trying to remain serious, Lumpy soon joined them, his belly laugh echoing deafeningly through the building.

With their glasses raised in toast, Zane exclaimed exuberantly, *"A la buena vida,"* and the men gorged and drank until dawn.

The ex-convicts soon discovered that life at the Hotel was not as hazardous as Lumpy had imagined.

Once the word had spread that the peculiar trio was straight, the rest of the hotel's entourage continued to treat them like they were one of their own. With an affinity for partying, the convicts joined their festive resort mates at most every event. They soon discovered that their gay brothers were a wild and highly entertaining bunch.

Most importantly, the three men felt like they were part of a family again, even if it was a perpetually bizarre and mildly dysfunctional one.

As the months rolled by, Zane finally felt like his old self. Since there had been no signs of Lesal or the police, the three men had quickly settled into their happy and carefree lives. Over time, they had become valued celebrities of the Hotel and their reputations for kindness and generosity had been acknowledged and appreciated by all in the secluded tropical oasis.

Five months into newcomers stay, the hotel staff decided to throw a party for their three honored guests.

The lobby and beach areas were lavishly decorated in festive rainbow decorations, and no expense was spared. Cases of spirits and a plethora of the finest local specialties were laid out, with techno music blaring mercilessly through a multitude of outdoor speakers.

The fest started at noon with a toast to Zane and his pals. With all glasses raised, Jorge, the hotel manager, spoke.

"Here's to my honored guests! You have brought new life and excitement to this small part of the world. We are throwing this celebration to show you how much we simply adore you all." With the heartfelt tribute finished, the crowd cheered wildly, and the party swiftly commenced.

Within hours, hundreds of exuberant people were partying on the beach.

Many of the local business owners closed their shops and joined the bacchanalian celebration. The fiesta quickly became a frenetic scene of dancing, drinking, and raucous laughter. Sweating profusely from the noonday tropical sun, Lumpy and Slim decided to leave Zane on the beach and retreated to the rooftop of the hotel.

Sitting under an umbrella with a bucket of iced beer, the two watched all the goings-on below.

Slim was the first to comment, *"This place really is fantastic. I had my doubts at first, but Zane had it pegged. The man is brilliant, and I have never been happier in my entire life."* Lumpy nodded in agreement as he raised a beer to his lips.

Watching the festivities below, Slim noticed an odd-looking man walking up the beach.

The short and stocky man was wearing a gaudy Hawaiian shirt and khaki shorts. Slim pointed him out to Lumpy, and they watched as the roly-poly tourist approached the party scene. Having a weird feeling about the stranger, Zane's pals decided to keep a close eye on him.

As Slim and Lumpy spied from above, the stumpy outsider milled through the crowd as though he was on the lookout for someone in particular. Finally losing interest in the out-of-place stranger, the drowsy pair sat back in their chairs. Hearing the start of Lumpy's raspy snoring, Slim pulled his hat over his eyes; the stifling heat and intoxicating brew insisting that it was time for a brief siesta.

Hearing the wild hoopla ahead, Lesal Spurnell had made a beeline toward the pulsating music.

For many months, he had been searching for Zane, to no avail. So far, all of his leads had been fruitless, and Lesal had concluded that Zane had thought very carefully about choosing the best hiding place to avoid detection.

As the months passed, the hunt had turned into a maniacal crusade of sorts. All the hitman wanted was to find his prey, dead or alive.

In his entire crime-filled career, Lesal had never come up against an adversary like Zane Worth. The man challenged him in ways he had never faced before. At the start, he had taken his target for a complete dolt, yet the outwardly brainless dope had managed to escape and elude him most effectively before his unfortunate incarceration.

When Lesal analyzed the details of the failed robbery in Norman, he realized that Zane had purposely botched the job just to be locked away behind bars. With Lesal hot on his tail, his wise pigeon had flown into the coop, not out. To the goons surprise, his slippery mark had figured out an ingenious way to get away from him and remain somewhat safe.

Lesal had been even more astounded when a paid informant, working as an Oklahoma prison guard had informed him that Zane had become the leader of the skinheads. In his estimation, only a highly savvy and ruthless criminal could have managed that coup.

After being apprised of the break-out, Lesal had been only a few days behind his target. Unable to unearth a single clue as to Zane's whereabouts, it seemed as though the escaped convict had simply vanished off the face of the Earth.

Something in the crooks' gut had told him that Zane had fled into Mexico, because it was the closest foreign country vast enough to easily hide out and evade US law enforcement for an extended period of time.

No matter where Zane was hiding, Lesal was bound and determined to find and recapture his elusive quarry.

As he scanned over the lively and colorful band of partiers, the gangster started feeling slightly ill at ease.

Most of the men were dressed in skimpy swim suits that revealed far more than Lesal was interested in seeing. Surprisingly, the women were even louder and more boisterous than the guys, and the whole party vibe seemed unusually wonky.

When he finally figured out that the majority of the crowd was gay, Lesal freaked out. Just as he was about to hightail it out, a young and highly enthusiastic lad dressed in an electric pink thong and matching feather boa grabbed the goon from behind. He clung tightly to the stumpy goon's backside, grinding seductively to the beat of a Bee Gees tune.

Lesal was mortified and quickly spun around, angrily pushing away his unwanted dance partner.

Assuming that his masculinity had been challenged, the hoodlum screamed out, *"Keep your fricken fairy hands off me!"*

His hateful words sliced through the air like a thunder clap, and the celebration came to a screeching halt. To Lesal's surprise, each and every person on the beach quickly surrounded him like an Apache war party.

Pushing her way through the crowd, an extremely large and hefty woman confronted the cantankerous hitman. Olga was on vacation from Sweden, along with her fellow female rugby team. Weighing in at three hundred plus pounds, Olga towered a good four feet over Lesal's head.

"Little runt, did I hear you correctly?" Olga inquired, with a deep and gravelly accent. The perpetually irritable criminal glared up at the blonde behemoth with a defiant sneer.

"You're all a bunch of worthless freaks, and if I had my way, I'd have you all lined up and shot," he screamed.

After dealing with loudmouthed bigots in the past, Olga smiled knowingly. Putting her face directly in Lesal's, she told him that he was no longer welcome at the party. Lesal scoffed loudly, then challenged, *"What are you going to do about it, you bloated buffalo?"*

Before Lesal could react, Olga drew back her brawny arm and planted an explosive punch. With no time to react, the irritating munchkin flew five feet into the air, landing face down in the sand. Unfortunately for Lesal, the mountainous woman wasn't quite through with him.

Ordering her fellow teammates to clear off a table, Olga picked up Lesal by the seat of his pants and splayed him unceremoniously across the splintery wood. Grabbing a string of party lights, she hogtied Lesal's hands to his ankles. As the crowd cheered her on, she carved out two pink ears from a papaya and jammed the fruity flaps on Lesal's head.

After propping up the comatose man's chin with a beer bottle, she shoved a large mango into his mouth, stating defiantly, *"If you are going to behave like a swine, you might as well look like one."*

Inspired by Olga's mockery, Jorge grabbed a corkscrew and jammed the handle into the crevice of Lesal's overabundant buttocks. Seeing the offensive stranger laid out like a luau boar sent the crowd into a decorating frenzy.

Each and every person quickly found something suitable to add to Lesal's unique décor. With a resounding cheer from the energetic crowd, the DJ put on some Hawaiian drum music and the crowd resumed their frenzied fete.

During his searching for Slim and Lumpy, Zane had missed the initial confrontation on the beach.

He finally found his buddies at the rooftop bar and had joined the pair for a round of Pena Coladas. Hearing all the fuss below, they had leaned over the rail, watching the whacky scene with confused curiosity.

Having no idea that there was a trussed-up mobster beneath the festive trimmings, Lumpy was the first to question, *"Oh my God, did they prepare a roasted pig?"*

Slim scratched his head, retorting, *"If so, we should get down there fast. I'm starving!"* The three men clanked their glasses in agreement and quickly made their way to the beach.

Lesal slowly awoke, his head pounding louder than the drum music accosting his ears.

As his eye's slowly focused, he found himself surrounded by

highly energized and completely inebriated people, who were dancing around him like whirling dervishes.

He tried to get up, but quickly realized that he was securely tethered. He tried to spit the fruit from his mouth, but it seemed to be permanently wedged in his teeth. With no means of escape, the hoodlum finally gave up trying. Wrapped up as tightly as a fresh bale of hay, he laid motionless on the table seething in uncontainable rage.

As the three tipsy friends approached the table, they were simply confounded.

Zane shouted for the music to stop and openly questioned the crowd as to why a man was lassoed like a rodeo steer and covered in food. Olga quickly appeared, retelling the entire hilarious story. Once she had finished, the crowd was astonished to hear Zane start to admonish them.

"I can't believe you all could treat another human being like this. I thought we were supposed to be better than that. This person is allowed to have his opinion, no matter how hateful it may be. Come on folks; let's show this ignorant straight man some compassion."

With an irritated scowl, he started to remove layer after layer of food and extraneous paraphernalia from the seething centerpiece. After removing the gooey papaya ears, he grabbed the mango and yanked it out with a resigned sigh of displeasure.

Finally uncorked, the stumpy hitman went on a blistering tirade. Blind with rage, he started chastising the entire group with unabashed profanity. When he had finally finished his scurrilous ranting, Lesal Spurnell looked up at the man who had un-gagged him and gasped.

At the exact same moment, Zane looked carefully at the irate stranger in disbelief.

Seeing that his quarry was just mere inches away, Lesal went completely bonkers.

"There you are you stupid son of a bitch! You're coming back with me to New York and finish the job you promised. And if you don't, I'm going to strangle you right here and now, in front of all of your limp-wristed friends."

Zane stared at Lesal as though he had seen a ghost. When he had recovered from the shock of seeing his nemesis again, he called his cohorts together. After a brief conversation, Zane strode confidently back to Lesal.

"Mr. Spurnell, I have grown utterly sick of you and your bad attitude. You have harassed me and my friends for the last time. To be honest, you are a despicable monster and deserve everything that is coming to you."

As Lesal watched in horror, Zane grabbed an empty beer bottle from the table and smashed it soundly over the gangster's skull.

As wild cheering echoed over the beach, the three convicts dragged the unconscious thug to the street behind the hotel. After locating his wallet and keys, they bound Lesal's arms and legs securely. Satisfied that he was going nowhere, they hid him inside a large canvas laundry bag.

Twenty minutes later, a service van pulled up, and the men pitched Lesal's limp body in the back. After paying off the driver, Zane slapped the side of the vehicle and it rumbled off noisily into the night.

At 2AM, the three friends were back at the rooftop bar, engaged in a heated discussion.

Both Slim and Lumpy were devastated when Zane informed them that his time in Mexico was up. With Lesal back on his trail, he knew it was time to move on.

Distressed at the thought of losing his best pal, Slim wanted to know why they hadn't just killed the aggravating nutcase. Zane explained that he couldn't live with the thought of a murder on his hands, even Lesal Spurnell's. Lumpy nodded and Slim took a big swig of his beer, asking, *"So, what are you going to do now?"*

Zane took a deep breath and laid-out the plan he had carefully formulated.

"I sent Jorge into town to find Lesal's car. When he gets back, I'm going to drive back to the US. With my new identification, I should be able to hide out easily without drawing attention to my true identity. No matter what, my archenemy will certainly start his search back here whenever he makes it back. If I move quickly, I will have a huge head start."

After musing over Mr. Spurnell's sticky situation, Lumpy chuckled evilly.

"Where that overfed tick of a man is going, it's going to be months before he shows back up here."

Zane and Lumpy quickly joined in the levity and the humid night air echoed loudly with waves of sarcastic laughter.

Slowly coming around, Lesal found himself trapped in a thick bag, with his arms and legs bound tightly. He could feel the motion of the vehicle and wondered where he was being taken. After struggling to free himself, he started screaming, *"If you can hear me you stupid jerk, you'd better stop this instant and let me out if you know what's good for you."*

When he realized his strident cargo wasn't going to shut-up, the driver slammed-on the brakes. Jumping out and opening the rear door, the man started beating Lesal with a baseball bat, shouting, *"Silencio, bastardo. Silencio!"*

After three additional encounters with the aluminum enforcer, the well bruised ruffian finally figured out it was wiser to just keep his mouth shut.

It felt like he had been on the move for weeks when the van suddenly came to a halt. Lesal heard the back hatch open and felt someone grabbing the bag.

Hitting the ground hard, Spurnell first cried out in pain, then cursed a blue streak. Seconds later, the ripping sound of a knife cutting through the sack was heard. Then miraculously, there was blessed light.

As his eyes adjusted to the glare, Lesal saw a strange man head toward the driver side door, soon returning with a familiar looking jar. Seeing his own bottle of chloroform sent him into a tizzy of anger, and he struggled wildly to free himself. The last thing he remembered was the driver holding a wet rag over his face and smelling the pungent odor.

Lesal awoke, face down in a pool of rancid mud.

All around him was jungle so thick that the trees totally blocked out the sun. To his horror, he realized that the only clothing he had on was a filthy pair of boxers. Rubbing his throbbing head, he called out, *"Yo, is anyone out there?"* Listening carefully, the only replies he heard were the ominous calls of chattering, yet unseen jungle inhabitants.

A few feet away, his eye caught something odd. It turned out to be a note sealed in a plastic bag. The handwritten message said, *"This is payback for giving Zane so much shit!"*

Instead of a signature, the message had a sketch of an unusually cheerful happy face.

Shaking his head in disgust, Lesal threw the note down and started following the faint tire tracts on the trail.

He trudged through the dense rain forest for hours, slapping and swatting at a blitzkrieg of attacking mosquitoes. To his dismay, each step seemed to draw him further into the confusing tangle of trees. After nearly stepping on a coral snake with his bare feet, Lesal solemnly swore under his breath.

"If I ever make it through this, I'm going to find you, Zane Worth. On that momentous day, you'll wish you were never born!"

Two days later, Lesal finally came upon a well rutted road.

With his blistered feet bleeding freely, and his body grossly swollen from a million insect bites, he forced himself to move onward. Just as he was about to give up hope, he saw a road sign ahead. Encouraged by the first hint of civilization, he sped up his pace.

When he was close enough to read the sign's message, the thug attempted to translate the words, "Bienvenido a Belice."

When the significance of the welcome sign finally sank in, Lesal fell to his knees in disbelief. Raising his fists to the sky, he screamed manically, *"I swear to God, when I find that despicable son of a bitch, I'm going to annihilate him. And I promise, it's going to be a slow and agonizing death!"*

CHAPTER 8
TOMBSTONE

CRUISING NORTH ON HI-WAY 200; Zane mulled-over the past two years of his life. Before initiating his moneymaking scheme, his former life had been pleasantly uncomplicated yet somewhat humdrum.

After encountering Lesal, his days had become a series of crazy adventures that he could have never foreseen in his wildest dreams. As he rolled through the varied terrain of Mexico, he came to a mind-bending realization. His existence had suddenly become meaningful and exciting, despite the fact he was constantly in fear for his life. He realized he had developed some much-needed self-confidence. Even in his dealings with Lesal, he had become far more assertive and daring.

Dwelling further on the subject of Mr. Spurnell, Zane knew he had an enormous head start. Without any identification, money, or clothes, he imagined Lesal was going to be stuck in the jungles of southern Mexico for an extremely long time.

Whenever he finally got his act together, it would be many months before Lesal would be back in Puerto Vallarta. If the mini mobster had any sense at all, he would avoid returning to the port city, knowing that the entire town would be on the lookout for the pint-sized curmudgeon.

Zane knew his only priority was to disappear off Lesal Spurnell's radar screen and lay low.

Since his early childhood, Zane had been enamored with tales of the Wild West.

Those early romantic depictions of gun slingers and wild saloons, with their be-feathered bar floozies and honky-tonk piano players, had always tickled his imagination. The first place that came to mind when he was first being chased by Lesal was to hide out in Tombstone.

After mentally debating his options, Zane finally decided to go with his initial gut instinct. Charting his course on the map, he guessed he would be arriving at the US border within four days.

After viewing many quaint and picturesque Mexican villages on his journey, Zane was shocked as he entered the outskirts of Nogales. Decrepit shanties littered the hillsides, and trash seemed to be strewed everywhere.

The only commonality that seemed to glue the community together was the unbreakable bond of poverty. Zane found the border town depressing, and his heart broke as he watched children playing in rusted out cars and mounds of uncollected garbage.

As he neared the American side, the city seemed less drab, but still looked rundown and grimy. Parking Lesal's car on a side street, Zane perused the area looking for a decent place to spend the night. On a hunch, he walked into an old Spanish style hotel constructed of adobe brick and decided it would do for an evening.

After paying in advance, the exhausted traveler started looking for a place to eat and toss down a few cervezas.

Picking out a quaint cantina, Zane sat at a table by the front window so he could watch the goings-on. Surprisingly, everyone seemed to be on a mission, and the overall spirit of the townsfolk seemed upbeat and festive.

Like most tourist towns in Mexico, there were armies of raggedly dressed kids hawking everything from religious paraphernalia to boxes of Chiclets.

The one thing they all had mastered was their overwhelming relentlessness in peddling their wares. Finally growing weary of the unending barrage of screaming children harassing him from the window, he moved to the bar, hiding behind a large statue of the Virgin Mary that had been placed strategically next to the cash register.

While savoring his Mexican brew, Zane finalized his plans for the following day.

Not willing to take the chance of driving across the border, he had decided to leave Lesal's vehicle parked in the alley. He was certain that the American authorities would check the car's registration. With the paperwork and insurance card in Lesal Spurnell's name, the irregularity might be difficult to explain.

Choosing the safer course of action, he planned on walking across the border to the American side. The bartender had informed him that there was a Greyhound terminal just a few blocks up from the crossing on the U.S. side, so Zane thought it would be wise to catch a bus to Tombstone.

With his future plans set, he sat back and started to unwind.

When it was time to retire for the evening, Zane threw the bar tender a fifty and told him to keep the change.

The stunned tabernero thanked him repeatedly for his generosity. Smiling mischievously, he tossed the keys on the bar as well, saying, *"My Lincoln has New York plates and is parked a few blocks down the street. If I'm not back in a week, the car is yours."*

Without looking back, he returned to his hotel.

After translating the vexing road sign, Lesal realized he needed to turn around and head back into Mexico. He walked for days without a car passing, or any signs of apparent civilization. With each and every excruciating step, he became more and more enraged.

Covered in foul-smelling perspiration and trying desperately to fend off the never-ending hordes of biting bugs, Lesal finally went into an uncontrollable rage.

Jumping and shaking his arms wildly, the agitated assassin cursed at everything he saw. He swore at the road, the trees, and the wild life, all while hopping around like an insane, enormous Mexican jumping bean.

He finally collapsed to the ground, absolutely exhausted from his overexertion. As he sat on the side of the road, gasping to catch his breath, something hard bounced off his head.

Both baffled and annoyed, Lesal picked up the marble-sized brown ball in wonder. He quickly looked all around, wondering where the projectile had come from. As he examined the odd-looking pellet, rolling it around with his fingers; another one hit him in the ear.

Looking up swiftly, all he could see were dense tangles of greenery rising to the top of the forest canopy. Still confused as to what was hitting him; Lesal squeezed the brownish ball and put it to his nose, quickly gagging at the smell.

Moments later, a tribe of howler monkeys started pelting him with a salvo of feces from the branches above. Both disgusted and incensed, Lesal scrapped up the monkey's ammo from the ground and attempted to return fire.

His counterattack proved to be completely ineffective, and only agitated the highly territorial Simians even further. Before he knew it, Lesal was being pummeled by an odoriferous hailstorm of poop. Quickly realizing he was fighting a losing battle; the gangster made a wise and hasty retreat.

As dusk started to settle in, Lesal heard the faint, yet distinctive sound of an approaching automobile.

Turning around, he saw an ancient Volkswagen bus traveling in his direction. Ecstatic upon seeing the first sign of humanity in many days, he started jumping up and down while signaling with his hands frantically. As the van approached the animated thug, it started to slow down. Lesal kept waving his arms wildly, not wanting the driver to miss seeing him.

Lesal was so overjoyed at his impending rescue that he started to dance an awkward jig of victory. Looking up to the setting sun with a maniacal grin, he swore, *"I'm coming for you Zane Worth. No matter where you run, I will find you and have my vengeance!"*

Without warning, he heard the sound of the van's motor revving unexpectedly, and the vehicle started to speed up. As dilapidated bus neared, Lesal saw a small child in the passenger seat pointing at him through the windshield, screaming, *"Mama! Chupacabra! …Vamonos!"*

With the tires throwing up dense clouds of dust, the van flew passed the con, nearly sideswiping him in a desperate attempt to get away from the jungle monster. Lesal was beside himself with anger. After flipping-off the vanishing rust bucket with both hands, he fell to his knees in all-consuming aggravation.

As the pissed-off mobster knelt in the dirt, trying to simmer down, his stomach started churning with severe hunger pangs.

Lesal realized he hadn't consumed a bite food in almost a week. With night settling in, he fought off his craving; figuring he could hunt up some food in the morning.

He pulled-off a dozen branches from a tree growing close to the road and constructed a makeshift bed. Hunkered up in his cocoon of foliage, Lesal Spurnell quickly drifted off into a dead sleep.

At dawns break, the jungle fauna started their raucous morning ritual of calls and the deafening racket awoke Lesal with a start.

After a prolonged stretch, he felt a strange burning sensation. When he realized that his skin felt like it was on fire, the thug panicked. Frantically pulling the greenery off his body, he realized he was covered in a blanket of army ants.

With a sharp yelp, Lesal leapt up and tore off his underwear, using the filthy rag to swat at the agonizing invaders. Now completely out of his mind, the naked stump of a man ran blindly down the road, shrieking like a deranged maniac.

In his frenzied escape, he almost ran over a pair of unusually small native men who were watching him flee in obvious astonishment.

The hitman stopped dead in his tracks, wondering if his eyes were playing tricks on him. As Lesal and the two jungle men stood motionless, starting at the other in wonder, one of the natives started rubbing his stomach.

"I'll be a son of a bitch! It would just be my luck to run into a pair of fricken cannibals in this hellhole of a jungle," was all Lesal could squeak out.

When both natives smiled and pretended to feed themselves,

the panicky hood gradually realized that they were simply offering him food.

Thankful beyond words that they weren't interested in eating him for dinner, Lesal nodded, mimicking with his hands that he was hungry. Grinning, one of the pair reached into his shoulder bag and pulled out a long, charred object, gesturing to Lesal that he should eat.

"What in hell is that?"

As though the native understood Lesal's question, the man replied, *"Lagarto."* Having no idea that the jungle men were offering him a roasted Iguana tail, the dubious city slicker tasted the odd-looking fare with suspicion. After the first infinitesimal bite, Lesal tore into the reptilian meal with ravenous abandon.

As he devoured his meal, his new friends were immersed in a muted discussion. To Lesal, their language sounded crazy and completely foreign. Leaving him to his dinner, the diminutive pair disappeared into the forest, returning a short time later.

In their hands were a crude and oversized loin cloth made of animal skins and a pair of sandals fashioned out of braided vines.

The naked hoodlum gratefully accepted the gifts, quickly trying on in his new jungle ware. Once dressed, they motioned for Lesal to follow them. Without a moment's hesitation, the desperate goon followed his lilliputian benefactors into the thick tangle of growth.

The odd trio hiked for several weeks, finally approaching the outskirts of a mid-sized community. As Lesal peered past the jungles edge, he saw buildings in the distance. When he turned to thank his rescuers, they had long since vanished back into the rain forest.

As quickly as the natives had disappeared; he could still hear the pair laughing hysterically in the undergrowth.

Desperate to get back into civilization, Lesal yelled out *"thank you"* and started running toward the city with all the strength he had left.

As the sparsely clad goon approached the main thoroughfare he tried to wave down motorists for help. Driver after driver sped passed him, honking their horns wildly. To Lesal's amazement, no one would stop and help. A few minutes later, he saw a police car approaching with its lights flashing. The officers quickly stepped out of their vehicle and nervously pointed their weapons at him.

In a fit of anger, Lesal started shaking his fists at the lawmen. After all he had been through, he was not going to let a couple of half-witted Mexican lawmen stop him from getting help. Screaming at the top of his lungs, the mobster dared them to fire.

Wearing a look of abject terror, one of the policemen fired his Taser gun, nailing Lesal squarely in his chest.

When Lesal slowly came to, he found himself locked in a holding cell. When he shouted out loudly for help, a burly guard appeared, instructing him in broken English to keep his voice down. Understanding the swarthy officer's warning, Lesal almost started to cry. After many months in the jungle, he was finally in a place where he could be understood. The grateful gangster whispered, *"Where am I?"*

"Chetumal, Mexico," was the gruff reply.

Zane rose before first light, anxious to be starting his new life back in the States.

After showering, he quickly dressed, carefully stuffing his cash into his underwear to avoid detection by the border authorities. After downing a cup of strong coffee in the downstairs cantina, he made his way to the street.

He stopped at the first tourist trap he encountered, buying a bagful of cheap souvenirs. Now satisfied that he looked like a typical sightseer, Zane made a beeline to the border crossing.

As he stood nervously in the declaration line, he prayed that his new passport would fool the immigration officers. If not, he was certain they would arrest him, then ship him back to a Mexican prison.

When he finally made his way to the front of the line, the border agent asked him curtly what was in the bag. Zane handed it over and the customs official examined the items carefully, then shook his head in amusement.

"You have very bad taste, even for a tourist," the officer stated with a chuckle.

Zane smiled innocently as the border guard scanned his passport. *"Everything seems to be in order, Mr. Maximilian. I hope you enjoyed your stay in Mexico."*

In another fifty steps, Zane was back on native soil. Throwing his bag of unwanted paraphernalia into the nearest garbage can, he walked to the bus station with a supercilious grin.

Two hours later, he arrived at his final destination. After checking into a roadside hotel, Zane grabbed some fast food to tide him over until morning.

Picking up a local newspaper from the front lobby, Zane sat on his bed, drinking coffee and scouring the job ads.

With few viable jobs available, he circled an unusual option, *"Gun slinger for Wild West reenactment needed. Applicant must be willing to fall twenty feet off a two-story building twice a day. Good pay and benefits."*

By the end of the week, Zane had been hired on to work as a desperado in mock gun battles at the local tourist trap in the center of Tombstone.

The staged show was simple, yet highly entertaining for the tourists, especially the awe- struck children.

Dressed in black, the evil sidewinders were all waiting in ambush, while Sherriff Wyatt Earp challenged the leader of the gang to a shoot out on the street. At the appropriate moment, a gun battle would ensure with the Sherriff and his posse eventually gunning down all the villains.

Zane was stationed on top of the saloon and was the first bushwhacker to be shot. Once hit by Earp's bullet, He would slowly fall off the roof with a dramatic scream, landing on a stack of mattresses hidden in the ally below. The entire show only lasted a few minutes, and Zane's impressive death plunge always evoked ooh's and aah's from the amazed crowd.

In-between skirmishes, the gun slingers would have the opportunity to schmooze and flirt shamelessly with the tourist. Other than working in the blistering heat of the desert, the job was relatively simple and gave Zane the chance to interact with other people.

At the end of the day, he would hop into his pickup truck and head for a trailer he had rented a few miles out of town.

As the sun slowly set in the west, Zane would watch the spectacle from his rickety porch while downing a sixpack: enjoying the intricate play of ever-changing colors in the darkening sky. To be sure, it was a simple existence, and Zane felt settled and protected in his new desert surroundings.

A few months into his new profession, Zane started chatting with a fellow employee named Nella Swimbura who worked as a saloon girl for the show agency.

As they got to know each other better, Nella finally came clean, admitting that she had fled from Baltimore to avoid serving a sentence for petty larceny. Flabbergasted, Zane confessed to his illicit past as well, telling her his entire unbelievable story.

After chatting with his new coworker further, he discovered that most of the locals were hiding out in Tombstone for one nefarious reason or another.

As the months passed, Zane and Nella spent more and more time together.

This raised the ire of Nella's old boyfriend, Errol Cajo. Errol played the part of Wyatt Earp in the show, and after performing the good guy lawman part for many years, had let the lead role go to his head.

After watching his ex-girlfriend and Franco smooch at the bar, Errol confronted the pair.

Annoyed by his rude and brutish behavior, Nella let Errol know that she wanted no part of his misplaced affections. Infuriated at her rejection, the jilted lover warned Nella's new beau that he had better watch his back. Zane laughed, stating confidently he wasn't the least bit afraid of the phony baloney Sheriff.

After storming out of the saloon, ranting and raving, Errol started scheming over underhanded ways to get rid of his hated competition for good.

A few months after the lovers skirmish between Errol and his rival, Zane was starting the second show of the day.

He had taken his place behind the saloon sign and was waiting for his cue to come out with his gun blazing. Once the shooting started, Zane emptied his revolver and leapt from the roof in his spectacular dive.

As he looked down, he realized that the pile of mattresses needed to break his fall were nowhere to be seen.

Lesal was trapped within an insurmountable dilemma.

With no identification, or money for bribes, his highly corrupt jailer refused to release him. He was allowed one phone call a week. Due to the antiquated, broken-down Mexican phone system, Lesal could never get through to his mob boss. Week after week, his long-distance calls were first met by crackly static, followed by complete silence. With his five minutes over, the guard would drag the prisoner back to his cell, kicking and screaming.

All Lesal Spurnell could do was sit alone in his claustrophobic holding pen and wait for the next opportunity to make a call. By the end of his second month of captivity, the crazed hood was going out of his mind.

Day after day, he sat brooding in his dank and filthy pen, mumbling over and over, *"If I ever get out of this stinking dungeon, I'm going to find that scheming little bastard. When I'm through with him, the man is going to wish that he had never crossed me! Come hell or high water, I will have Zane Worth's head on a platter."*

When Zane awoke, Nella was looking down at him with a troubled expression. As his brain cleared, he vaguely remembered jumping off the saloon roof, but the rest was a hazy blur.

"Jeezus, what happened to me?" Zane asked groggily.

"That evil bastard, Errol, removed your mattresses and you fell

straight to the pavement," Nella sobbed. *"The surgeon tried to save your arm, but…"*

As she spoke, Zane quickly looked to his left and turned white as a ghost. Where his arm had once been, was now just a bandaged stump.

"…he couldn't. To save your life, they had to amputate it." Nella whimpered.

Zane never heard the last part of his girlfriend's grim message since he had already passed out from shock.

After the loss of his arm, Zane plunged himself into a sea of self-pity.

For a man who was once extremely proud of his handsome good looks and athletic physique, he now felt broken and incomplete. Without falter, Nella stood by her man, always trying to give him much needed reassurance and hope.

Months after his recovery, Zane and Nella were sitting on the porch of his trailer enjoying the crisp morning air.

She had been reading the job ads section of the paper out loud with her partner listening disinterestedly. Zane knew his gun slinging career was now history, and he wasn't sure what a one-armed man could do to earn any kind of living.

Attempting to cheer him up, Nella read an absurd sounding ad.

"Notice: We are holding an international conducting competition to employ a new music director for the Tucson Philharmonic. All qualified candidates must submit a resume for review to receive an opening on the roster for the audition."

As she laughed over the absurdity of her lover being an orchestral director, Zane perked up and asked when the auditions would take place. *"You've got to be kidding!"* Nella scoffed. *"What makes you think you could conduct a group of professional orchestra musicians?"*

For the first time in a very long while, Zane smiled widely. *"And why not?"* he bantered back. *"I still have one good arm, and with a name like Franco Maximilian, I'm a shoe in for the job!"*

As his partner howled with laughter, Zane kept scheming.

"Nella, I think I really could do it. I played trombone in high school until I dropped out, but I really loved the band. All I need are some music books, and a few old video tapes of a famous conductor like Leonard Bernstein. In a few months, I could conduct as well as any of those pompous numbskulls."

When Nella realized he was being dead serious, she tentatively agreed with his plan, even though she secretly thought that he had completely lost his mind.

After a quick round trip to Tucson, she returned with an armful of materials on the subject, and Zane dove into the books and videos with unrestrained excitement.

After a week of practicing Bernstein's conducting technique in front of the TV monitor, Zane was convinced he could pull the off the scam. He quickly drafted a bogus resume claiming he was the associate conductor of the Orquesta Symphonic de Bilbao.

With his Spanish sounding name, Zane was hopeful that no one in would delve too deeply into his musical pedigree.

A few weeks later, Zane received a letter confirming an audition time in Tucson. Running to Nella in a tizzy, he couldn't stop repeating, *"I told you so!"*

The musical selections for the audition were Mozart's *Overture to the Magic Flute* and the opening movement to Beethoven's *Fifth Symphony*.

Zane was ecstatic when he realized that both works were on his videos. With two weeks before his audition date, Zane started studying day and night, mocking each and every move he saw Bernstein make.

When taking a break from his conducting studies, he would practice his phony European accent. Zane was going to be well prepared to pull the wool over the Tucson Philharmonic's eyes.

A few days before his conducting debut, he performed his entire concert routine in front of Nella. She had to admit it was a very convincing mockery, and for the first time in weeks, she started to believe that he might be able to pull off the Music Director charade successfully.

They drove to Tucson the day before the audition to buy Zane a new suit and a few conducting batons. For the rest of that evening, Zane practiced conducting in front of the mirror like a man possessed until the wee hours of the morning.

CHAPTER 9
THE DEBUT OF MAESTRO
FRANCO MAXIMILIAN

THE MORNING OF THE conductor auditions, the Tucson musicians had slowly started to file-in to work. Unlike their overly excited management team and board members, to them it was just another day of drudgery.

To the group's collective dismay, the winner of the audition would eventually become their new leader, and no one in the ensemble was particularly thrilled at the prospect of dealing with a highly temperamental and unpredictable new boss.

A new conductor always opened up a whole new can of worms for the ensemble.

Wanting to duly impress the board and audience, the overeager music director would be full of novel ideas and would push the players ruthlessly to work harder. In a few weeks, highly disruptive work politics would surface; with the ensembles toadies running to the new boss with their personal gripes and complaints.

The unusually jaded band of musicians were well known for being a vengeful bunch, and many mindless feuds between excessively combative players had gone on for decades. With a fresh and unacquainted conductor, there would be renewed opportunities for disgruntled musicians to seek avowed reprisal.

Christoph Fowler was a grizzled veteran within the Tucson orchestra's ranks.

What the principal clarinetist lack in musical proficiency, he made up for in political power. After forty years of tenure, the ill- tempered performer headed the orchestra committee, and was a relentless pain in the ass for the ensembles management team. None of the associations business proceeded without Christoph's sole approval, and he ran the orchestras affairs with ruthless efficiency.

As he put his instrument together, Christoph scanned over the list of prospective candidates. When his eyes came across Franco's name, he paused.

"Crap," he mumbled under his breath. *"The last thing we need here is an arrogant, Spanish dictator."*

With a resigned sigh, he started going over the more difficult passages in his music.

After fumbling miserably over the few solos he had, the irritable clarinetist made his way to the green room for a much-needed cup of coffee.

As he walked offstage, Christoph brooded over his dismal morning warm up, thinking arrogantly, *"What the hell, it's more than good enough for this sorry-assed group."*

As he searched for his oversized mug, with the words "Principal Clarinet Rules" splayed across it, he shared his thoughts about a new conductor with the first oboist who was soaking his reeds in some water.

Rorig Bonnad had also played in the symphony for decades and was another incorrigible curmudgeon. What Christoph had never seemed to understand was that Rorig disliked the man intensely. As the clarinetist babbled on, the disinterested oboist stared back at him impassively, wondering as to when the talentless buffoon might suffer a brain aneurysm and die an agonizing death.

Most every individual in the philharmonic seemed to have had a long running grudge with another player in the ensemble. Over the years, those hardcore feuds had grown and festered, becoming full-blown psychotic manias.

Hatred and retribution had become the orchestra's collective obsession. Unfortunately, it was far too late for anyone to quell the massive waves of loathing that would soon wash over the stage in a tsunami of catastrophe.

Zane had been assigned a dressing room downstairs, and with Nella's assistance, put on his new suit and tie.

After looking into the mirror, he sighed despondently. The coat sleeve of his left arm hung down, waving like a flag in the breeze. Seeing Zane's sorrowful gaze, she quickly slapped him on the back of the head, scolding, *"Stop feeling sorry for yourself. You look great, and I won't put up with anymore of your self-pity."*

Realizing that his annoyingly optimistic partner was absolutely right, Zane grabbed his scores and started conducting along with the music playing in his head with new found zeal.

By the luck of the draw, Zane Worth had been the last candidate on the list. When he finally heard his named being called, he jumped up from his chair and took a deep breath. With his fingers crossed for luck, he followed the personnel manager onto the stage.

As Zane looked out over the sea of unfamiliar faces, he noticed that most of the musicians looked bored to tears, and a few, visibly irritated. When the tactless ensemble saw the one-armed conductor take the podium, a few open snickers could be heard.

Boldly raising his baton, he started the overture with unabashed flair and verve.

The orchestra quickly responded, taken aback by his confidence and energetic leadership. When the movement had ended, Zane bowed his head in deference to the professional ensemble.

For an uncomfortable moment there was dead silence. Slowly, the sound of subdued applause arose from the musicians. Seconds later, he heard raucous clapping coming from a highly enthusiastic woman in the audience.

Members of the symphony board had been watching the conductors from the auditorium, making their own assessments of each candidate.

When Zane had taken the podium, one patron in particular had taken great interest in him. Her name was Ms. Regina Sableslider and she was a most formidable character. Using her vast fortune to meddle in worthy causes, she held great influence with every nonprofit organization in Tucson.

What Regina wanted; Regina got; and anyone who desired her financial assistance genuflected obediently to her capricious demands.

The moment he had taken the podium, Regina had fallen head over heels for the dashing and handsome Spanish conductor. By the time Zane had finished conducting, she had already figured out how land her prize. Wearing an egotistical grin, she calmly passed a note to the CEO of the Tucson Philharmonic.

When he opened the paper, the man almost choked. It was a

check made out to the association for one million dollars. On the back of the check was a clear and concise message.

Hire Franco Maximilian immediately.

When Christoph Fowler heard the news of Franco's appointment as Music Director, he went ballistic.

He knew that a young and brash foreign Maestro would insist on everyone in the group performing their parts perfectly. Painfully aware that his playing was in a steep decline, Christoph went on red alert. He wasn't going to give this wet behind the ears, Spanish-born bozo a chance to criticize him.

The clarinetist had planned to go on the offensive and vowed not to give this new Music Director any slack. He was sure, that after a few days of rehearsing, Mr. One-Armed Bandit Maximilian would quickly figure out who the real boss of the ensemble actually was and leave him alone.

As he mentally prepared himself for the first week of the symphony season, the cranky clarinetist plotted ceaselessly, coming up with a multitude of devious methods to derail this new threat to his crumbling career.

Zane was astounded when he heard the news of his appointment as Music Director. In the back of his mind, he was certain that he had placed dead last at the audition.

When the realization hit home that he would have to conduct twelve concert series, as well as manage the musical performances of every musician in the group, he felt weak in the knees.

Nella tried to bolster his waning confidence by telling him that almost every classical work known could be viewed in concert form on the internet. As he studied the upcoming music he would conduct on the web, Zane realized that Nella was correct. It was all online for him to review and emulate. As he started watching videos of the music for the first week's concert, a shrewd smile crossed his face.

Zane felt like he had a good chance of pulling off the biggest musical scam of the century.

On the fateful morning of the first orchestra rehearsal, both Zane and Christoph had thoroughly prepared for the momentous day.

The practice started well, with the group responding cooperatively to Zane's few minor requests.

A few minutes before the rehearsal break, Mr. Fowler played an abysmal solo that put a screeching halt to the rehearsal. Even a novice like Zane could tell that the clarinet was terribly out of tune, and unacceptably strident in sound.

After a brief pause, the young conductor asked the aging clarinetist to play his part alone.

Christoph had been waiting for this moment with unbridled glee. He quickly stood up, and informed his new boss that he was a consummate professional. He went on to claim that his solo had been played perfectly.

When Zane politely disagreed, the clarinetist flew into a tirade.

"What would a second-rate European conductor know about American clarinet playing? If you don't like working with this country's musicians, perhaps you should ship yourself back to Spain where you belong."

At that point, Rorig had heard enough of Christoph's unjustified harassment.

The oboist had listened to cantankerous clarinetists verbal assaults for years and had finally become fed up. He stood and turned to his despised colleague, telling him in no uncertain terms that he needed to shut up and retire for the musical sake of the orchestra.

Already hot under the collar, Christoph started screaming insults at Rorig, and the two almost came to blows.

Not exactly sure how to handle to the contentious situation, Zane stood frozen on the podium.

He had never seen somewhat rational people act in such a rude and insulting manner. As the two musicians continued taking underhanded pot-shots at the other, Zane called for the break to start. Not wanting to miss a single scandalous insult, the entire orchestra sat glued to their chairs, mesmerized by the confrontational pair trading malicious slurs.

In an attempt to retake control of the situation, Zane shouted, *"If you both don't stop this at once, I will fire you both on the spot."* Upon hearing the new conductor's warning, the entire orchestra quickly focused their attention to the man on the podium.

As a novice music director, Zane had absolutely no experience in dealing with orchestral psychology. If he had, he would have understood that once you threatened one musician, you had inadvertently threatened them all.

In the orchestra's eyes, Zane had instantly become the enemy and the entire ensemble glared at him with unmasked contempt. One by one, the peeved musicians slowly filed offstage in hate-filled silence. It was perfectly clear to everyone in the room that the clueless Maestro had made an unpardonable misstep.

While sipping on his cup of coffee, Christoph was gloating openly.

He was highly confident that he had conquered the new boss on day one. Yet, he could not be certain of his success until the break was over to see if Franco would avoid correcting him again. If there were no further comments about his performance abilities, the clarinetist knew he had won the coveted battle for supremacy.

Regina had been sitting in on the rehearsal to watch her newest artistic acquisition. She became livid upon seeing how the orchestra had turned on her conductor without rhyme or reason.

She quickly shuffled her way to the front of the stage, calling out for Franco. When he bent down, she whispered into his ear, *"It's your orchestra, so do what you think is best."*

Encouraged by his patron's support, Zane remained on the podium, pretending to study his score while planning his next move.

Marching solemnly back to the stage, the musicians were in an obviously foul mood. They had been discussing the disconcerting conductor situation heatedly for the past twenty minutes and had stirred themselves into a complete lather.

After Rorig gave the tuning A, Zane instructed the ensemble to start where they left off. Unfortunately, that was exactly where Christoph had his solo. As expected, the clarinetists performed his part horribly, his caustic notes almost peeling the paint off the walls.

Zane stopped the group and politely asked Christoph if he could play the music in tune, in time, and with a pleasant tone. The principal clarinetist immediately arose in a huff.

"How dare you! I don't have to take that kind of mistreatment from the likes of you."

Zane smiled wisely, informing the musician that he needed to go home and practice.

As Christoph remained standing in defiance, the confident conductor let the crabby clarinetist know that if his performance wasn't markedly better the next rehearsal, he would be dismissed permanently.

Christoph simply could not believe his ears. His bluff had been called and he wasn't sure what to do next. Throughout his entire lack-luster career, his excessively aggressive demeanor had kept him from having to face up to his own lack of ability.

Feeling the eyes of the orchestra fixed on him, the musician sputtered angrily, *"I swear upon my mother's grave, I will have you fired for this outrage!"*

CHAPTER 10
LESAL'S LAMENT

LESAL SPURNELL WAS COMPLETELY confounded by the situation he was facing. For months on end, he had tried to contact his mob boss, but to no avail. After countless attempts, he finally gave up trying.

After being locked up in his cell twenty-four hours a day and given nothing but pinto beans and rice for his meals, Lesal grew fatter and fatter. His captor had refused to provide him with any hygienic care, so his hair had grown long and become wildly matted. His teeth quickly yellowed, and decay had rapidly set in. To his consternation, Mr. Spurnell had slowly turned into a squat, yet enormous, fur covered beast, barely recognizable as a human being.

Noticing how bizarre looking Lesal had become, his jailer started charging admission to the locals to view the "fea bestia de la selva." Lesal became an overnight celebrity, and once the word had spread, people started coming from all parts of the region to witness the ugly jungle beast for themselves.

To keep the audience from hearing Lesal's desperate pleas for help, the police chief had enclosed the front of the cell in Plexiglas. Before the morning show, he would use a high-pressure hose to spray *the beast* down. Of course, this would infuriate the mobster and he would jump around his cell screaming and cursing. Once his side show freak had become thoroughly agitated, the police chief would parade a line of well-paying spectators through.

When Lesal finally figured out what his captor's new enterprise was, he blew his top. His anger became uncontrollable, much to the bemusement of the amazed yet horrified on-lookers.

After months of swearing and screeching until he became hoarse, Lesal finally gave up. With his spirit completely broken, he sat quietly in his cell staring back at his inquisitive onlookers.

His jailer was not the least bit pleased with Mr. Spurnell's unexpectedly tranquil behavior.

In an effort to get his peso-making monstrosity to start moving again, he located a large hornet's nest and threw the entire colony into the cell. Within seconds, the infuriated insects were stinging Lesal without mercy, making him hop and scream about like an unhinged lunatic.

Satisfied with the results, the warden re-opened the jail for the impatient customers. The gangster soon realized that if he did not play the part of a crazy jungle man, he would be subjected to a variety of tortures by his captor. Resigned to his fate, Lesal started giving his audience the best show possible. In return, his jailer doubled his rations, and Jungle beast's body grew exponentially larger.

After months of demeaning exploitation, the crowds slowly faded away.

The townsfolk had finally grown tired of the obese, hairy oddity, and the police chief saw his profits shrink to a dribble. When he could no longer afford to keep Lesal fed, he sold him to a small traveling circus troupe.

With a rope around his neck and his legs shackled, the inhuman hairy blimp was dragged to his new home, an iron-barred cage mounted on a brightly painted cart with wheels. Lesal was lugged from village to village throughout southern rural Mexico in his circus pen. Totally powerless to free himself, Lesal would hunker down in the straw bedding each evening and chant repeatedly, *"Kill Zane Worth, Kill Zane Worth!"*

A few months into his demeaning circus career, Lesal was accidentally liberated by Mother Nature.

Camped near a tiny settlement a few hundred yards from the Caribbean coast, the show troupe had settled in for the night. Without access to current news, they were totally unaware that a major hurricane was rapidly approaching the area.

The bands of driving rain started around midnight, with the winds swiftly picking up in intensity. By 4AM, the full force of the storm was upon them. All the tents and equipment started to sail away, with the rattled carnies scurrying around trying to batten-down their precious property.

Lesal's cart was broken free from its mooring by the fierce winds, slamming violently into a palm tree. Noticing that the corroded bars had buckled, Lesal saw his chance to escape.

Kicking repeatedly at the bent part of the cage, the weakened bars finally gave in and Lesal managed to squeeze through the opening. With the storm's winds creating utter havoc, no one from the circus saw their blubbery ape man flee into the tangled growth of jungle.

Gales over one- hundred-fifty miles an hour turned loose leaves and debris into painful projectiles. Even the driving raindrops felt like unrelenting blasts of gravel fired from cyclonic cannons.

With trees falling all around him, Lesal Spurnell kept running, never once looking back to see if he was being chased. By the time the storm had passed, the exhausted gangster had collapsed, too weak to take another step.

As he lay prostrate on the forest floor, gasping for breath, Lesal set a plan in his mind. He would make his way north toward Cancun. If he could make it that far, he knew he would be able to find English speaking tourists who could help him.

Until he arrived at his destination, he would travel alone, avoiding any human contact. No way was Lesal Spurnell taking any chance of being recaptured and exploited by corrupt Yucatán entrepreneurs.

At mornings first light, Lesal started making his way north. He figured it would be easier to hug the coastline, quickly ducking into the jungle if he saw any locals.

By the end of the first week, the mobster wandered into a small hamlet nestled by the ocean's edge. Late in the night, he snuck into the town, stealing clothes off the lines and securing a five-gallon jug of fresh water.

When he heard a mongrel started barking wildly, Lesal escaped quickly into the undergrowth. With the dreaded memories of his recent confinements still swirling in his head, he ran as though his life depended on it.

A few days later, he stumbled across a large fishing village. A dozen boats lined the beach, with a handful of men unloading the evenings catch. Lesal hid behind a cluster of palms, watching the fishermen secure their crafts for the evening. After seeing an opportunity to speed up his escape, he revised his scheme.

Under the cover of darkness, he crept up to the boats, looking into each one to see if any were stored with provisions. Finding a small skiff with a couple of ten-gallon gas canisters of fuel inside, he pulled the craft stealthily into the water. Once afloat, he found a long oar and pushed the boat out past the breaking surf.

Mouthing a silent prayer, he pulled on the outboard motor's rope and the engine quickly purred to life. Gunning the throttle, he pointed the boat into the open sea.

Lesal didn't start to relax until the flickering lights of the fishing village had disappeared past the horizon. As he rummaged through the storage bins, he came across gallons of fresh water and plenty of food staples.

For the first time in over a year, the gangster smiled.

He was sure he had enough fuel to take him to Cancun, plus adequate provisions to keep him alive throughout the lengthy trip.

He looked up to the starry night sky and thanked God for his help. If he made it back to civilization, he promised the Creator above he would quit the mob and even start attending church.

Grateful beyond words for his good fortune, Lesal Spurnell had become a changed man.

As he sat in the stern, steering the craft northward, he heard the sound of a rolling bottle on the floor beneath him. Reaching under the seat, Lesal pulled out a bottle of homemade tequila.

Like a child on Christmas morning, he tore into the unexpected gift and started chugging the throat burning brew. Long before he had made his way to the bloated worm at the bottom, the mob assassin had passed out in inebriated bliss.

A cold splash of water awoke the hefty hoodlum from his drunken stupor. Shaking out the cobwebs in his head, he realized that he was trapped in the middle of a violent thunderstorm.

With lightning cracking around his head, Lesal frantically donned a life jacket.

When the angrily frothing waves started to break over the bow, he held on to the craft with all his strength. The last thing he remembered seeing was an approaching wall of water towering twenty feet over his head, illuminated by a blinding bolt of electricity.

Shaking his fist angrily, he cursed God for his fickle cruelty. Not the least bit amused by the mobster's bad attitude, the spurned and vengeful Deity tossed Lesal violently out of the boat, and into the churning sea.

CHAPTER 11
INSIDIOUS SCHEMES

CHRISTOPH FOWLER WAS BESIDE himself with anger. After being insulted and threatened by the upstart new Music Director, he was in a very foul mood. By the time he exited the parking lot to head home, he was totally out of his mind with rage.

Weaving in and out of traffic like a lunatic, he shook his fist and flipped off every motorist he felt was in his way. By the time the clarinetist had arrived home, he was even more aggravated than when he had left.

Once inside his apartment, he quickly called the local musicians union.

He was sure that someone there could help him stop the Maestro from harassing him. After a very brief discussion with the steward, Christoph slammed the phone down in disgust. He had been informed that he was on his own, and that there were no rules or regulations against conductors asking musicians to simply play better.

Completely flustered, Christoph ran to his computer.

He hoped a web search of Franco Maximilian would turn up some information that he could use against his newest archenemy. To his amazement, only a few matches turned up and none of the people listed were conductors. With a sigh, the clarinetist entered Spanish conductors into the search area. This time, not one single mention of Franco Maximilian appeared.

The total lack of information stunned Christoph, but he hoped with a bit more research, he could find the ammunition he needed to destroy the mysterious Maestro.

Sifting through the web, he found the number of a private investigator that specialized in uncovering information on suspicious people.

After giving him detailed instructions, they settled on a fee. The manic musician made it crystal clear to the detective that if he did not come up with any solid leads on the Maestro, he wouldn't pay him a red cent.

His last call of the day was to the orchestra's personnel manager, purposely calling in sick for the next for the next two weeks.

With his homework finally complete, Christoph smiled smugly and mixed himself a large cocktail. He was positive that by the time he had to return to work, he would be fully armed and ready to do battle with the accursed new Music Director once again.

Rorig Bonnad sat at his kitchen table seething over the disturbing events of the day.

The oboist was furious at Christoph for drawing him into the morning rehearsal free-for-all. As he thought back over his many years of playing in the ensemble, he realized how much he despised the dreadful musician. For decades, he had put up with clarinetist's cutting jabs, cantankerous personality, and horrific playing.

Because of Christoph's recent contemptible behavior, Rorig felt his career had now been placed in jeopardy.

As he stewed over the situation, he finally concluded that he needed to take care of his pesky problem, once and for all. Contemplating Christoph's demise brought an instant smile to his face, and Rorig started formulating ways to eliminate the clarinetist without being caught.

After brainstorming for a few minutes, he suddenly jerked up with a plausible idea coming to mind. *"Yes,"* the oboist mused evilly. *"This is definitely going to Mr. Fowler's final season."*

Laughing psychotically, Rorig opened a bottle of Gin and filled his glass to the top. After slamming-down the liquor with gusto, he mumbled threateningly, *"My dear Christoph, you should have never piss-offed this oboist! Now you shall reap you just reward."*

Errol Cajo had been browsing through the newspaper before work.

His jaw dropped in disbelieve when he read of Franco's appointment as conductor of the Tucson Philharmonic. As he scoured the article, he became more and more agitated. The dishonorable sidewinder had inexplicably recovered from his diabolical trap and had landed on his feet with a prestigious job.

Errol was beside himself with resentment. His warped code of honor had been violated, and his ego, severely crushed. He sat at the bar mulling over possible ways of getting back at his sworn enemy. With thoughts of revenge swirling in his brain, the bogus sheriff suddenly grinned.

As he strutted out of the bar for the morning gun battle, he swore under his breath, *"Franco Maximilian, prepare to be buried in Boot Hill!"*

The persistent lapping of the surf at his feet awoke Lesal from his stupor.

Slowly rolling over, he realized he was lying on a deserted beach. As his brain cleared, he recalled the ferocious storm and the gigantic wave that had propelled him into the raging sea. Grateful to be alive, he closed his eyes, letting the balmy ocean breeze dry out his waterlogged clothes.

As he basked in the sun's warmth, he heard an odd click from behind him, and then another. Sitting up quickly, he turned around to see two men in green army fatigues pointing their rifles at him. Stunned at the sight, Lesal mumbled out a weak hello and asked where he was.

With a thick Spanish accent, one of the soldiers responded, *"Cuba,"* followed by, *"You are under arrest for being a US spy."*

CHAPTER 12
LESAL SPURNELL'S TORMENT
AND REDEMPTION

AFTER SEVERAL MONTHS, LESAL was finally allowed to meet with a representative of the US State Department. After telling his fraught-ridden tale of capture, and fortuitous escape from Mexico, the astounded ambassador promised that he would do all he could to get Mr. Spurnell released and back to America.

The Cuban penitentiary that Lesal was locked up in was infamous for its treacherous inmates and brutal guards.

With little money allotted for food, the half-starved prisoners were allowed only three small scoops of rice a day. The ravenous goon had to fight like a savage to keep the other inmates from stealing his meager rations.

Within weeks, Lesal was starving. He had never felt so hungry, and his mind constantly obsessed on how to find more food.

Late one evening, Lesal awoke to find a gargantuan rat chewing on his big toe. While most people would have jumped out of their skin in horror, the goon pretended to remain asleep. Then, with lightning swiftness, he lunged down. After snaring the rodent, he held it by its throat, watching it struggle and squeak in desperation.

As he toyed with his prey, his mind focused in on Zane.

With a crazed look in his eye, he vowed, *"You did this to me you bastard. If I ever get out of here, this is what I'm going to do to you."* He grabbed the rats head and slowly twisted until it dislodged. With an insane howl, he started chewing ravenously on the rodents raw flesh.

In one unfortunate food scuffle, his opponent had pulled out a hidden shank, slashing Lesal from the top of his forehead to the end of his jaw. The wound became grossly infected and had healed badly, leaving the mobster's face deeply scarred, and drooping to one side.

After losing all hope of being liberated, Lesal Spurnell slowly sank into total madness.

Eight months into the gangster's prison stint, the state department finalized Lesal's release. When he arrived at LaGuardia airport, even his crime boss failed to recognize him.

The moment Lesal stepped out of the terminal gate, he fell to his knees and started kissing the heel-scuffed linoleum.

When he saw his boss in the terminal lobby, he ran into Axel's arms, feeling more joy than he had ever felt in his life. Finally recognizing his subordinate, Mr. Gilan put a reluctant arm around Lesal and helped him walk to their awaiting limo.

On the ride back to Brooklyn, Axel overheard the goon mumbling a bizarre mantra repeatedly. *"Must find Zane Worth…*

Must kill Zane Worth!" When the mob boss asked Lesal what he was rambling about, the mobster just started laughing hysterically.

After realizing Lesal had taken a swan dive off the deep end, the mob boss made the necessary arrangements to have the gangster committed.

CHAPTER 13
THE MAESTRO'S FIRST CONCERT

ZANE WORTH HAD REHEARSED the orchestra relentlessly for a full week. With Christoph out of the picture, the group had settled-in, and the music was starting to come together nicely.

Rorig could not have been happier. With the distracting clarinetist home with the blue flu, the entire woodwind section had started to blend, and for the first time in decades, to make ear-pleasing sounds.

Regina Sableslider had attended each and every rehearsal, becoming more and more aroused by her sexy new conductor. As she watched the object of her intense desires go through his paces, Regina started plotting of a way to mount her prize stallion.

Minutes before the concert was to start, Zane had a major panic attack.

The thought of thousands of audience members watching his performance had finally hit home. Sweating profusely, Zane could barely get his clothes over his drenched body. Nella tried to comfort him as best she could, but nothing she said seemed to provide him with much comfort.

With his stomach churning, and his hand shaking uncontrollably, Zane walked to the podium in a daze.

As he was about to give his opening downbeat, someone in the audience stared to cough raucously. The unexpected distraction threw off his concentration, and Zane spun around to the audience with a glaring look of disapproval. Entirely stunned, the audience responded with a collective inhalation.

Flustered by his uncontrolled reaction, Zane quickly turned back and started the overture with an overly dramatic gesture.

The orchestra instantly responded to his energetic direction, and the music took-off at breakneck speed. Knowing that the piece was going far too fast, Zane tried to slow the music's speed down, but the orchestra ignored him completely. The group plowed ahead with reckless abandon, with Zane trying desperately to keep his arm beating with the tempo.

When the overture ended, there was a momentary hush.

The silence was quickly broken by Regina screaming out *"Bravo!"*, quickly followed by thunderous applause from the astonished audience. It seemed that the unexpectedly brisk tempo had energized the crowd, and they quickly rose to their feet, giving their fiery new Maestro a standing ovation.

With his in initial unexpected success, Zane's confidence quickly blossomed.

By the end of Beethoven's 5th symphony, he was conducting with sparkling flair. Before the resounding final chord had sounded, the audience was again on their feet, the applause almost deafening. Zane turned to the crowd and bowed graciously, then motioned for the orchestra to join him.

Sitting directly behind him, Regina shouted loudly for Zane's attention. When he bent over to shake her hand, she pulled him down, planting a lingering and passionate kiss on his lips.

From her seat in the balcony, Nella watched the brazen

spectacle playout below in alarm. She made a mental note to find out who the bejeweled Jezebel was, and to put a halt to her obvious advances.

After the show, Zane was shaking hands with the exuberant audience members, whose line went far past the stage entrance. An hour later, Zane was finally through thanking his well-wishers. When he entered his dressing room to change, Nella and Regina were inside, glaring coldly at each other.

When Regina questioned Zane as to who the other woman was, Nella quickly responded, saying she was his partner.

Ignoring the woman completely, the wily heiress again questioned her conductor, asking if he was married. With the mood of the conversation quickly growing contentious, Zane laughed uncomfortably, saying that as of yet, he had no ring on his finger.

Regina smiled coyly. *"My dear Nella, it looks like Franco is fair game and from what I can see, you simply don't have much of a chance of keeping him from me. After all, why would he choose a beat-up jalopy like you, over a Mercedes Benz like me?"*

Before Zane could intervene, Nella punched Regina squarely in the nose.

In seconds, the two green-eyed competitors were on the floor, angrily slapping and pulling each other's hair.

Zane tried to stop the brawl, but the two continued to claw and scratch with animalist abandon while screeching at the top to their lungs. Finally, the security guard broke-up the seething pair, with Zane at a loss as to how to handle the delicate situation.

Regina broke the icy silence first.

"Franco, I shall give you the final decision in this matter. If you

pick me as your partner, I promise that you will retain your job with the orchestra. Or you can remain with that lowlife floozy and return to your mundane and tragic former life. The choice is yours, but you need to demonstrate your intentions this very instant."

Zane remained silent, trying to figure out what to say next.

He love Nella dearly, but his new life was now in great jeopardy. If he rejected Regina, he knew he would soon be back in his ramshackle trailer, slowly wasting away in Tombstone. Drawing a deep breath, he kissed Nella gently on her cheek, then whispered softly, *"I'm so very sorry."*

As Nella stood dumbstruck with disbelief, Regina grabbed hold of Zane's arm and dragged him toward the stage door. As the conniving heiress passed, she looked back at Nella with a triumphant sneer. Then, with a haughty chuckle, she paraded her newest conquest to her waiting limousine.

Fighting back her tears, Nella watched despondently as the automobile disappear down the dimly lit street. She could not come to grips with the fact that Zane had dumped her for Regina. Gathering up her shattered self-esteem, the jilted woman walked slowly toward her vehicle.

As Nella turned the ignition key, she suddenly stiffened in anger. Infuriated by Regina's despicable manipulations, she swore to have her comeuppance.

"No matter what it takes, I will get my man back from that two-timing rich bitch," she sputtered. *"Regina Sableslider, you had better watch your spineless back."*

CHAPTER 14
RORIG ENACTS HIS PLAN

CHRISTOPH FOWLER WAS BESIDE himself with frustration.

After weeks of relentless research, he kept coming up short on any information pertaining to Franco Maximilian. Even his hired investigator had been stumped. It seemed like the enigmatic Maestro had sprung out of thin air, without any traceable past.

Knowing that he couldn't afford to take any more time off of work, the clarinetist was petrified of his pending return to the orchestra. He was sure that the upstart conductor would berate him over his unexcused absence, and still insist that he play better.

The only chance he had was to somehow turn the orchestra musicians against Franco Maximilian again. Unfortunately, after the rave reviews in the Art's and Leisure section of the newspaper, the unpredictable ensemble had quickly dropped their brief grudge, and were now openly ecstatic about their new Maestro.

Letting out a resigned sigh, Christoph got into his car. Already sick to his stomach with worry, he slowly made his way to the hall for the morning rehearsal.

With his despicable nemesis out sick for past two weeks, Rorig Bonnad had been in sheer heaven.

After seeing how wonderful it was to have Christoph temporarily out of the picture, he had worked diligently, thinking of ways that would make Mr. Fowler's absence permanent.

After carefully mulling over his options, he knew that shooting the foul clarinetist between the eyes was out of the question. That would draw unnecessary attention to him, and quite frankly, Rorig was terrified of guns. No, Christoph's death had to be slow, to some extent painful, yet totally undetectable.

As the oboist methodically searched the web, he came across an interesting article. Slowly smiling, he copied the material. Yes, Rorig mused: poison was the perfect solution to his dilemma. Cackling like the Wicked Witch of the West, he started reading through the text.

From the information he had gleaned, cyanide was his best bet. In its diluted form, the deadly chemical was almost tasteless, yet would slowly buildup in the body, inevitably shutting down all of Christoph's internal organs.

The biggest problem was how and where he could obtain the deadly mixture.

Rorig was certain that you couldn't walk into your local drug store and order a gallon of cyanide without having to answer a lot of self-incriminating questions. As he researched further, he discovered that silver and gold mines used the toxic chemical in the ore refining process.

After memorizing all the information, Rorig walked to the gas fireplace and started a large blaze. Once the ceramic logs had heated up sufficiently, he placed his printed notes and the laptop into the inferno. If his plan to poison Christoph was successful, Rorig Bonnad was taking no chance of having investigators digging through his electronic equipment for evidence of his damning research.

After an evening concert, the oboist changed into his street clothes, then drove due south. At 3AM, he was standing outside the chain link fence of a gold mining operation near Bisbee. Using heavy-duty wire cutters, he clipped out a hole in the wire big enough to climb through.

Once inside the property, Rorig stumbled across a decrepit storage shack. After kicking open the rickety wooden door, he entered cautiously. Using a flashlight, he combed the sheds interior searching for the murderous concoction.

In the back corner were several shelves with large containers marked NaCN. Knowing that he would only need a small amount, Rorig, pulled out an empty milk jug from his duffel and poured out a gallon of Christoph's liquid demise.

With a sadistic gleam, he scurried back to his car and headed for home.

Back in his apartment, Rorig grabbed a used water bottle. He drew out some of the cyanide, putting a teaspoons worth into the container. He added some tap water and shook the contents well. With a smug sneer, he put the tainted water bottle in his work bag and happily wandered off to bed.

The past two weeks of self-induced stress had taken a harsh toll on the clarinetists system.

Parking his car in the hall garage, Christoph's gut felt like a raging inferno inside. He had been looking forward to this fateful morning with all-consuming dread. If the Maestro was displeased with his lack of improvement, he would be put out to pasture in great shame.

The boiling in his bowels was almost unbearable as he sat in his chair in preparation for the doom-filled rehearsal. Rorig was next on stage, arriving early to test his latest batch of reeds. When their eyes met, the two men glared at the other, with neither one offering a civil greeting.

After a few minutes, and no longer able to bear the intestinal distress, Christoph flew out of his seat and ran to the restroom.

The second he was out of sight, Rorig grab the clarinetist reed soaking glass. Opening his cyanide-laced water bottle, he replaced the liquid in Christoph's reed soaker with his lethal concoction. Positive that nobody had seen him, he hid the rest of poisoned mixture back in his bag. With a grin of pure evil, he quickly pulling out his knives and went to work whittling on his reeds.

Looking white as a ghost, Christoph returned ten minutes later. He dropped his reeds into the water cup and put his clarinet together. After adjusting his best reed to the mouth piece, he played a few notes. Quickly stopping, he grumbled, *"This reed tastes like almonds."*

Momentarily distracted by the poisons distinctive aftertaste, the clarinetist went back to work, fumbling frantically through the first piece on the rehearsal order.

While Christoph honked away on his instrument, Rorig sat back in his chair wearing a malevolent smirk. He knew it could take weeks, or possibly months, but sooner or later, Christoph would succumb to his subterfuge. Until his dastardly plan came to fruition, the oboist would watch carefully for signs of his dirty work, while basking in his well-deserved payback.

CHAPTER 15
NELLA AND ERROL MAKE PLANS

DEVASTATED BY THE DISASTROUS turn of events, Nella had crawled back to Tombstone with her tail between her legs. Outmaneuvered by Regina, and castoff by Zane, she sat alone in the trailer for days trying to sift through her feelings.

By the end of the week, she had returned to her job back at the saloon and buried her emotions in her work.

When Errol Cajo found out she was back in town, he flew to the bar hoping to reunite with his lost love. Nella wanted no part of Errol's affections and made her feelings crystal clear. No matter how hard he begged, his former lover ordered him to go away and leave her alone.

Brooding at the opposite end of the bar, Errol swore to avenge his ex-girlfriend's honor. He reckoned that if he could eliminate his heartless nemesis, perhaps Nella would acknowledge his inextinguishable love for her and take him back. It seemed worth a try, and Errol started to finalize the evil scheme in his head.

As he chugged his beer, a smile slowly broke out on his face. Mumbling with foam-ringed lips, he vowed, *"Franco, you're as good as dead!"*

Nella was busy making some plans of her own.

She was certain that Zane still loved her, and if Regina could somehow be taken out of the picture, she would have her man back. The more she thought about the situation, the angrier she became. She despised Regina and knew that the rich old cow needed to pay dearly for her duplicity.

One day during work, Nella slowly walked up to Errol. She put a hand on his shoulder and asked coyly, *"Can you teach me how to shoot a gun?"*

Errol was both stunned and beside himself with joy. He promised that within a month, she would be the best shot in Tombstone. Nella smiled grimly, then quickly responded, *"Good, let's start practicing tomorrow morning."*

Thinking that he might have a glimmer of a chance to get Nella back, Errol cheerfully promised, *"I'll meet you for practice in the OK corral at 6AM."* The saloon gal nodded affirmatively and strolled back to her waiting customers.

Nella Swimbura secretly planned to use Errol's gun expertise to her advantage, and nothing would stop her from completing her noble quest. *"Regina,"* she swore under her breath, *"It's time to see if your worthless blood is really blue."*

CHAPTER 16
LESAL SPURNELL'S RECUPERATION

THE WHACKED-OUT MOBSTER SPENT the next six months at the Raven Hill Psychiatric Clinic. Bound in a straitjacket and confined to a padded cell, Lesal ranted and raved incessantly about a mysterious, yet unbelievable character by the name of Zane Worth.

His doctors worked tirelessly trying to convince their berserk patient that Zane was just a figment of his imagination. They had identified his delusions as some sort of post-traumatic stress disorder stemming from his trials in Mexico and were stubbornly sticking to their diagnosis.

After months of fighting vehemently with the staff, the mobster realized that the only way he was going to get out of the nuthouse was to play along. He forced himself to relax and stop arguing, and slowly but surely, the doctors started seeing some improvement in their ballistic patient.

Lesal did everything in his power to convince his doctors that he was indeed getting better. His civility finally paid off when his doctors determined that he was ready to be unbound.

Once they had removed his straight jacket and placed him in a community ward, Mr. Spurnell started working on arts and crafts projects as part of his anger therapy.

From bowls to vases, he dove into his new passion with verve. Even his doctors were impressed with his knack for shaping very artistic pieces and urged him to continue exploring his newfound creative side.

With a moronic grin plastered on his face, Lesal cheerfully agreed with his captors, while thinking inwardly, *"I'll show you how inspired I can be."*

Several weeks later, the mobster presented the entire staff with their own personalized coffee mugs. Unaware of the thug's criminal cunning, they happily thanked Lesal, while being duly impressed with his thoughtful generosity.

Unaware of the goons devious plan, Lesal had used a lead-based glaze to decorate their cups. Instead of fully firing the pieces, had had partially baked the mugs knowing that the lead would quickly leach out into the boiling hot coffee.

If any of the staff members absently forgot to use their mugs, the hitman would immediately go into a mock depressive state. Not wanting to impede Lesal's progress, the director of the asylum issued a memo instructing everyone to use the handmade earthenware at work.

Within a few months, the entire medical staff started complaining of splitting headaches and feeling unusually fatigued. Lesal watched everyone's health slowly deteriorate with contained glee. By the end of his institutional confinement, all of the personnel were making exceedingly poor judgment calls due to undiagnosed symptoms of lead poisoning.

After losing most all of their reasoning powers, the highly irrational physicians called a meeting with Mr. Spurnell and asked him if he felt prepared to reenter society. With a sincere expression, Lesal said that he felt cured and was anxious to start his new life.

After the proper forms were signed, the conniving con artist was released from Raven Hill with a clean bill of health.

Once freed, Mr. Spurnell went back to work for his boss, for who he owed quite a bit of money. Lesal performed his usual tasks; breaking kneecaps, strangling deadbeats, and capping unfortunate lowlife's who had foolishly tried to weasel out of paying their debts to the mob.

When his work day was over, Lesal would head home and wolf down a quick meal. After a prolonged hot shower to wash away the sickly-sweet stench of death, the gangster would make his way to his bedroom. In the corner, he had set up a command center with TV monitors and several computers, all connected to the internet. On the wall above the electronic equipment were enlarged photos of Zane with ice picks and switchblades imbedded into his forehead.

Every evening, Lesal would actively hunt down any leads to the whereabouts of his elusive counterfeiter. He scanned newspaper articles, listened to police chatter, and scoured the internet looking for any sign of Mr. Worth.

His obsession over locating Zane kept him fairly sane, and he looked forward with evil delight to the moment he could resume stalking his prey.

Anytime he felt the least bit discouraged in his quest, he would look up at the photos of Zane and vow, *"I know you're out there somewhere, and some day, I will find you. As God is my witness, I will abduct you and make you pay dearly for my undeserved suffering. When that glorious day comes, I will torture you like no one's ever been tortured before. When I have finally found sufficient satisfaction in your prolonged agony, I will slice open your chest open and tear out your beating heart with my bare hands."*

CHAPTER 17
FRANCO MAXIMILIAN'S
CAREER BLOSSOMS

Zane was amazed at how well his new career as an orchestra conductor was progressing. He started studying all the classical music publications, as well as boning up on videos of all his future concerts. In a short period of time, he was well versed in all aspects of the classical music world and seemed to be able to fool even the savviest musical connoisseur.

Regina used both her affluence and influence to promote her new play toy.

From San Francisco to New York City, she paraded her handsome conductor from musical event to event. With the woman's relentless promotion and personal fortune, Zane became the newest conducting sensation. His fame started spreading like wildfire and orchestras around the country started clamoring for him to conduct their ensembles.

There was one downside to his new life that was highly disturbing. Zane was tied to the hip by his overbearing and highly manipulative partner twenty-four hours a day.

Not wanting Franco out of her sight for a second, she had sequestered him to her palatial estate in the foothills north of Tucson, and he was only free to leave if Regina accompanied him.

She made one fact abundantly clear to her unenthusiastic partner. If he mistakenly strayed from her side, the partnership was over, and he would be thrown to the wolves. She promised she would destroy his career in a heartbeat, and if provoked, she could have him "disappear" without anyone the wiser.

Now, fearing for his life, Zane simply gave up on any notion of trying to reconnect with Nella and quietly acquiesced to his new boss's ever-shifting desires.

The Tucson Philharmonic musicians had been bolstered by their newfound fame, and their collective performances became more refined. Other than the perpetually floundering French horn section, there was only one musician who seemed to be playing with decreasing accuracy.

Christoph was in a total panic.

Both his playing abilities and health now seemed to be in a rapid decline. Growing weaker by the day, he had initiated a health-conscious diet, and started practicing his instrument for hours every day to retain what little facility he had left.

To his consternation, no matter how much effort he put into the clarinet, his playing continued to plunge downhill at a remarkable pace. Recalling the continual dour looks coming from the podium, he was convinced that the Maestro was planning to fire him at any moment. Well aware that being dismissed by the snooty conductor would completely destroy his monumental ego, he redoubled his efforts to improve in a frantic attempt to remain in the group.

To the entire orchestra's dismay, Christoph's clarinet playing had started sounding much like a dozen cats being shredded alive in a cotton gin. The howling and wailing became so corrosively abrasive, many of his colleagues had resorted to using ear plugs to cope with the painful cacophony.

No matter how many times Zane commented on Christoph's appalling performance, the clarinetist grew progressively worse. When Christoph had a solo passage, Zane would just close his eyes and grimace.

Bowing to the principal clarinetists incessant demands for action, the musicians union had been forced into reprimanding the egregious conductor for his slanderous diatribe and had stubbornly supported Christoph's continued tenure. With the union president waiting to pounce on him with legal actions, Zane had to be extremely careful not to blatantly criticize the abysmal player.

It had become perfectly clear to all concerned that nothing short of an act of God was going to remove Christoph Fowler from the stage.

As Christoph's health and playing deteriorated, Rorig Bonnad was beside himself with delight. Although Mr. Fowler's offensive clarinet playing had becoming unbearably excruciating, he knew it wouldn't be long before the crappy clarinetist dropped dead.

Before every rehearsal, Rorig would spike the clarinetists reed water with his deadly concoction, then sit back in silent amusement. Quite frankly, Rorig had been somewhat surprised that Christoph had lasted this long. Becoming increasingly impatient, the vengeful oboist had doubled the dose of cyanide in Christoph's water, making it the deadly concoction far more toxic.

Rorig Bonnad knew it was just a matter of time before his foul deed would bear tasty fruit. As far as the heartless oboist was concerned, he was reasonably sure that Christoph Fowler was already living on borrowed time.

By the middle of the symphony season, the Tucson ensemble was playing to sold-out houses.

With Regina's connections, the National press started taking notice of the brash and dashing, one-armed conductor. With rave reviews being published in every city's newspaper, Franco Maximilian quickly leapt into the national public eye.

One early Sunday morning, Regina walked into the bedroom with a tray of coffee and a periodical, smiling like the cat that ate the canary. When he glanced the cover, Zane almost fainted. There, from head to toe, was his picture plastered of Time Magazine.

The last thing he needed was national publicity and prayed that no one would be able to see-through his new identity. Zane went pale at the thought of Lesal Spurnell catching a glimpse of his face on a news stand and had an uncontrollable urge to choke the life out of Regina for exposing him to the world.

When his benefactor asked conceitedly what he thought her most recent coup d'état, Zane mumbled back sarcastically, *"That's just what I needed, my dearest."*

For the first time in many months, his stomach started twisting in acidic knots and his paranoia had resurfaced with a vengeance.

If Lesal was able to put two and two together, he would be back on the hunt in seconds. With all the recent press exposure,

Zane realized it would be next to impossible to hide from the ruthless goon. With a drawn-out sigh, he resigned himself to the fates and hoped that his hell-bent bloodhound wasn't much of a classical music fan.

Nella had also seen the Time magazine cover.

After reading the article on Franco at the saloon's bar, she had broken down, crying over the loss of her world-renowned lover. A few minutes later, Errol walked in, catching her sobbing uncontrollably.

The sight of Nella's emotional pain infuriated him, and he knew he needed to act quickly to win back the object of his desires. As he exited the saloon, he made a pledge to himself. Franco Maximilian would suffer in endless agony for destroying his girlfriend's fragile heart.

Days after the Time Magazine issue was released, Zane was immediately thrust into the epicenter of the musical world's spotlight. Within hours, telegrams were coming in from every professional ensemble across the planet wanting him to conduct.

With Regina acting as his business manager, she started to negotiate engagements with the managers of every major orchestra from Hong Kong to Vienna.

To Zane's horror, the entire world's eyes seemed to be watching his every move.

CHAPTER 18
THE CONCERT OF THE CENTURY

THE TUCSON PHILHARMONICS' FINAL concert program of the season had been finalized.

Regina had chosen the music herself to springboard Franco's international debut. Every notable music critic had been invited to the gala, as well as the press corps from every national news organization. The orchestra had rehearsed for months in preparation for the highly anticipated event. Zane had labored tirelessly to ensure that all the musicians played their parts to the best of their abilities.

There was only one major problem blocking Zane's successful performance.

Regina had unknowingly picked the one piece on the concert that could possibly derail the entire event. She had insisted that her favorite piano concerto, *Rhapsody in Blue*, by George Gershwin was to be performed. Although the jazzy American composition was a popular and crowd-pleasing favorite, the opening of the work started with a monumental clarinet solo.

Every time Christoph would attempt to play the difficult opening glissando, the clarinet had sounded more like an unhinged hyena than a bonified musical instrument.

After repeating the passage a half dozen times during the final rehearsal, Zane simply gave up, hoping that the miserable clarinetist might beat the overwhelming odds against him and play the part somewhat acceptably at the concert.

The second half of the concert extravaganza was Tchaikovsky's *1812 Overture.* The iconic Russian masterpiece always wowed the audience with its bombastic flair, and Regina wanted the work to be Franco's symphonic cannon shot heard around the world.

Ten minutes before the concert was to begin, Christoph Fowler sat on stage, quaking in his chair.

His mind was swimming with panicky thoughts, and he felt deathly ill. Unable to take a proper breath, and feeling overwhelmingly woozy, the clarinetist tried over and over to get his solo to sound passable. Fortunately for Christoph, the excited chattering of the entering audience members drowned out his ungodly caterwauling.

The clarinetist recognized that tonight was his last chance to redeem himself in the eyes of the Maestro and his fellow orchestra members. If he failed at his task, he had decided to retire voluntarily and put away the clarinet forever. Christoph's entire musical career now hung on how he performed tonight's tricky solo passage.

Upon hearing the tuning A, Mr. Fowler felt like an elephant was sitting on his chest. The pressure was almost too much to bear and the room had started to slowly spin around him.

As the house lights dimmed, the Maestro turned to Christoph with an unmistakable look of impending doom. With the audience hushed in anticipation, Zane took a labored breath and gave the calamitous clarinetist his cue to begin.

Nella Swimbura was making the final preparations to her disguise before driving to Tucson.

She had come to the determination that something had to be done straight away if she was ever going to be reunited with her stolen lover. After seeing all the publicity on Franco, she knew that he would soon be leaving Tucson for conducting engagements around the world. If Zane was leaving the United States soon, it was not going to be with man stealing tramp, Regina Sableslider.

After donning her fanciest red dress and designer shoes, she grabbed a Colt 45 revolver and stuffed it in her purse. Placing on a fancy hat and some dark sunglasses Nella looked at her reflection in the mirror smugly. With a threatening growl, she vowed, *"Regina, this is going to be one concert performance that's going to knock your socks off."*

Climbing into her truck, she began the two-hour journey toward her uncertain destiny.

Nella wasn't the only person from Tombstone planning to attend the final Tucson gala concert. Errol Cajo had also secured a ticket for the highly promoted event.

Earlier that day, he was putting on the final touches of makeup to disguise himself. After looking carefully in the mirror, he started to roar with laughter. He had put on a woman's grey wig and a fancy ball gown to disguise his true identity.

After stuffing himself into the frilly dress, he styled the wig into a huge wave on the top of his head. After placing a cheap, gaudy tiara atop his overflowing quaff, he was convinced that he looked like any other matronly battle-axe that would attend the high-class musical event.

While finishing his primping, Errol mentally reviewed his scheme to kill Franco Maximilian.

He had secured a place in the front row of the balcony near the exit. From that position, he was sure to have a clear shot to the front of the stage. His plan was to shoot Franco just before the end of the final piece, and then escape before anyone realized what had happened.

When he entered the hall in Tucson, the ill-plotting assassin made his way upstairs to the balcony. After seeing the lengthy distance between his vantage point and the podium, Errol prayed that his shooting skills would not let him down. Trying to calm his nerves, he settled into his seat and watched the other concert patrons as they entered the auditorium.

His eyes suddenly focused-in on a shapely, well dressed woman making her way to the middle of the second row. With her fancy hat, glittering scarlet gown, and designer sun glasses, Errol thought she looked like a high-class movie star.

If he had known the woman's true identity, he would have quickly rethought his murderous scheme.

Nella made her way to the front of the auditorium searching for her seat. She had secured a ticket in the second-row center, with her payback in mind. She knew that Regina always preferred to sit in the first row, directly behind Franco. If she had planned her position correctly, Nella would be sitting directly behind the despicable inheritress who had shanghaied her dream man.

With her pistol safely hidden in her purse, she had planned to wait until the raucous Tchaikovsky finale.

When the cannon shots started, Nella was going to reach into her handbag and fire her weapon through the back of Regina's seat. She was sure that the sharp pop of her gun would be muffled by the bombastic barrage of noise on stage. After slaying Regina, she would quickly rise from her seat and exit the building before anyone was the wiser.

⊰⟫⟫⟨⟨⊱

With his big solo at hand, Christoph Fowler was on the edge of having a nervous breakdown.

He was visibly trembling and had never felt so ill in his entire life. With Franco's cue to start playing, he slowly drew the clarinet to his lips and struggled to take a deep breath.

At that highly inopportune moment, the poison finally completed its lethal mission and the clarinetist slumped in his chair, dead as a door nail.

With his instrument propping him up in his chair, Christoph looked as though he had simply fallen asleep at the wheel. Seeing his big chance to finally be heard, the scene stealing second clarinetist grabbed Christoph's music off the stand and started playing the solo.

Zane watched the bewildering scene in amazement, not realizing that Christoph had already left to meet his maker.

With the opening clarinet solo played well for the first time in decades, the remainder of the Gershwin work proceeded extremely well.

The orchestra performed enthusiastically, playing with all their heart and soul. At the end of the jazzy musical showcase, the entire audience leapt to their feet, applauding noisily for the electrifying music. Zane motioned for the ensemble to stand and join the soloist in a bow, with everyone in the auditorium clapped wildly.

Only poor Christoph remained firmly planted in his chair, slouched over his instrument, no longer amongst the living.

Having the curious feeling that something was amiss with one of the players, the stage manager quickly closed the curtain. Once all the musicians had shuffled off stage for intermission, Zane and the stage crew slowly approached Christoph.

Not sure if he was dead or just snoozing, Zane gently tapped the clarinetists shoulder to wake him. To everyone's amazement, the corpse collapsed to the floor with a resounding thud.

Shrugging his shoulders, the stage manager grabbed Christoph by his ankles and started to drag him offstage. Not wanting to leave the dead body in the wings where it might upset the other musicians, he stuffed the expired clarinetist into an empty string bass case and quickly slammed shut the lid.

Back in his dressing room, Zane was discussing the disastrous clarinet situation with Regina. Suggesting that it might be a good idea to call the authorities right away, Regina argued vehemently to wait until the concert was over.

"I don't want a minor mishap like Christoph's death marring my gala event," she scolded. *"We will wait until the musicians and audience have departed, then you can call the police if you wish."*

Knowing that there was no way to win an argument with the dictatorial woman, Zane nodded submissively, and the discussion ended.

"After all," she sang out sanctimoniously, *"The show must go on!"*

With the intermission break over, the musicians had filed back on stage to take their places.

Wondering where the principal clarinetist had disappeared to, you could see members of the woodwind section quietly gossiping amongst themselves. As he returned to his chair, Rorig Bonnad was glowing like a super nova. He had been waiting for this monumental day his entire career and had to stop himself from the overwhelming urge to shout for joy.

Zane started the *1812* show stopper with reserved care. Using his baton to caress the cellos opening choral, you feel the musicians emote under his poignant direction.

As the music started its carefully calculated crescendo to the battle finale, the Maestro started conducting with orchestra with uncontained bravura. Swooping and swaying wildly, Zane was determined to put on the best show of his life.

The musicians found his enthusiasm infective and the ensemble started playing with wild abandon. The hall started resonating with increasingly louder waves of raucous brass chords and sonic booms bursting from the percussion section.

When Nella heard the first thundering cannon shot, she opened her purse and secured the pistol inside.

Watching the back row of musicians carefully, she fired her pistol into Regina's back at the precise moment an overenthusiastic percussionist slammed a gargantuan bass drum with his mallet. With the battle scene raging on, the music was so loud that even Nella had missed hearing the deafening blast of her gun.

She watched Regina twitch sharply, and then drop her head to one side. Satisfied that her target was hit, Nella quickly stood up and started making her way to the end of the row.

Presuming that the end of the musical battle scene was near, Errol had quietly gotten out of his seat and moved next to the exit door. Hidden in the shadows, he took aim on the despised conductor.

Mumbling a quick prayer, Errol steadied himself and fired his weapon directly at Zane.

Unfortunately for Nella, she had risen from her seat at very moment Errol had taken his first shot. The bullet pierced her between the shoulder blades, and she fell over Regina's corpse.

When he saw that he had missed his target, Errol cursed the lady in red, and then started firing at Zane in desperation. The second bullet passed through the conductor's dangling left coat sleeve and buried itself in Rorig's Bonnad's shoulder. The oboist dropped his instrument and fell onto the principal flutist. When the irritated woman pushed Rorig off of her in disgust, she saw his gushing wound and screamed in horror. Unfortunately, the earsplitting music effectively covered her terrified wails as well.

Highly befuddled, Zane watched as musicians inexplicably started dropping from their chairs. Not knowing exactly how to react to the bizarre situation, he kept conducting while frantically wondering what in blazes was going on. At the end of the work, he quickly turned to the audience and bowed deeply. The crowd leapt to their feet with wild applause.

Over the shouts of *"bravo!"* a much more menacing sound started to grow. With a handful of musicians obviously bleeding out on the floor, the remaining members of the orchestra quickly realized that a someone had been taking potshots at them and started screaming in horror.

The ensemble started to stampede off the stage, trampling over their slower colleagues in a desperate attempt to reach the exit. When the audience members witnessed the chaos on stage they panicked as well, and soon the entire auditorium was immersed in chaotic bedlam.

Zane stood immobile on the podium in utter confusion. His world debut had instantaneously turned into a catastrophe, and he had no clue as to what had caused all the mayhem. Becoming furious, he stormed offstage to his dressing room, positive that the insane finale to his gala concert was going to put an instant kibosh on his career.

With Regina nowhere to be seen, Zane assumed she had left with the rest of the crowd. Furious with his flighty subjugator for leaving him behind, he ordered the stage manager to call him a cab.

When the highly distraught manager asked him what he was supposed to do with Christoph's body, Zane screamed, *"Throw him the trash receptacle outside where he belongs!"*

As the taxi headed toward Regina's estate, Zane questioned the driver as to why there were so many police cars racing toward the downtown area with their lights flashing. The cabbie commented back, *"Jeez, something really bad must have happened!"*

Zane laughed sarcastically at the retort, replying, *"Yea. They are probably looking to arrest me on the charge of homicide… for murdering my own career."*

After fleeing the concert hall, Errol Cajo sped south down I-17 like a bat out of Hell.

No longer able to justify his actions rationally, his mind became trapped behind an impenetrable veil of denial. The final events of the evening had happened so quickly that he wasn't exactly sure what had happened. By the time he had reached Tombstone, he felt thoroughly confused and disoriented. He vaguely remembered firing his weapon at Franco and killing him, but after that, his memory had gone totally blank.

Completely convinced that he was the reincarnation Wyatt Earp, Errol refused to believe he had done anything less than honorable. However, the last shred of his sanity prudently decided that it might be wise to lay low for the next few weeks. Once all the hubbub had died down, Errol would return back to work and attempt to rekindle his relationship with Nella.

With Franco out of the picture permanently, he had every reason to believe that she would happily take him back.

CHAPTER 19
A SUPER STAR IS BORN

EARLY THE NEXT MORNING, Zane sat at the breakfast nook, still fuming over his botched concert. He wondered what the ever-impulsive Regina was up to since she had not returned home after the show.

After starting the coffee maker, he grabbed the newspaper from the front step and opened it up to the Art's and Leisure section. As he waited for his brew, he started looking for a review of the performance. Finding nothing reported about the disastrous concert event, he happened to flip to the front page, and his jaw dropped. The headline read *"1812 Overture battle scene insights a massacre."*

As he read further, he couldn't believe his eyes. Listed among the dead were Nella Swimbura and Regina Sableslider. There were three other seriously wounded musicians who had been caught in the line of fire. Ten additional musicians were hospitalized after being stampeded over by their panic-stricken colleagues. Later on in the article, there was an additional report on an expired clarinetist, cause of death yet determined.

The paper went on to say that an unidentified elderly woman sitting in the balcony had inexplicably opened fire during the final moments of the concert, and a manhunt was now on for an armed and dangerous grey-haired female in her late sixties or seventies.

After recalling his past experience with Lesal disguised as an old woman, Zane gasped. He wondered if the mob goon had caught up with him and had been waiting in the wings to exterminate him. As he mulled over the possibility, he started to relax.

"No" he finally reflected. *"The mobster would have definitely tried to torment me first. Since I haven't seen any of his obnoxious calling cards, I can be relatively sure the killings were not his doing."*

As Zane read the eye witness accounts of the concert bloodbath, he shuddered.

He realized how close he had come to losing his own life. With his brain in such a blur that evening; he hadn't realized that so many people had been killed or injured.

As he thought about Nella's demise, a tear rolled down his eye, and waves of remorse racked his body. With the meddlesome Regina dead as well, he had lost both his one true love and irksome financial benefactor. Again, his life had quickly become familiarly bleak and uncertain.

While Zane pondered over his questionable future, he heard some commotion in the courtyard.

Opening the front door, a dozen reporters started screaming out questions, as cameras flashed, and video recorders whirled. Stunned, Zane just stood there with his mouth agape. Tongue-tied and highly embarrassed, he quickly slammed the entry way shut. Collapsing against the back of the door, Zane wondered how he was going to get out of this extremely undesirable situation.

The press remained stubbornly outside Regina's house, waiting for Zane to re-emerge. Not wanting any more exposure than necessary, the humiliated Maestro hid inside the estate, staring at the TV news coverage of his front door. After several days of unrelenting surveillance, the media finally gave up and started looking for more interesting stories to cover.

With Regina's money no longer at his disposal, Zane was quickly in need of cash. With the prying eyes of the reporters and paparazzi gone, he called a cab and headed to the Symphony office to pick up his paycheck

When he arrived, the secretary instantly smiled seductively. Completely ignoring her obvious advances, he demanded that she roundup his check at once. When the scowling woman returned, she was holding dozens of telegrams along with his pay check. After a harsh look of distain, she dropped his mail to the floor and walked away in a snit. Zane picked up the mail and quickly scanned the messages. In seconds, his heart started racing.

There were offers from orchestras around the globe begging for him to conduct. To his amazement, the fees the managements were offering were enormous. Zane stashed all the offers into his pocket and hurried off to the bank to cash his check.

Certain that he would soon be thrown out of Regina's house by her money hungry heirs, Zane loaded the limo with all his possessions. With a heavy heart, he ordered the driver to head back to his rundown trailer in Tombstone.

Hunkered down inside his dilapidate doublewide, Zane started making plans to reinvent his career. He knew it would be a long time before the Tucson organization would be able to reopen its doors. The law suits alone would take years to run their course. The unemployed Maestro now had no choice but to accept outside engagements.

In an ironic twist of fate, the tragic circumstances in Tucson had turned into a greater opportunity for Zane. With his pending foreign engagements, he would no longer need to rely on Regina's financial assistance or be blackmailed into sexual servitude. Once out of the United States, he would not have to dwell over Lesal Spurnell, or anyone else who could possibly expose his questionable past.

Zane realized that booking a world tour to conduct renowned foreign orchestras was the wisest plan to escape from all of his worrisome entanglements.

CHAPTER 20
SHOOTOUT AT THE OK CORRAL

AFTER CONTACTING THE MANAGEMENTS of a dozen well known orchestras, Zane had successfully booked a series of international concerts from Beijing to Berlin. With his future plans set, he had started to breathe easier, knowing that his life would be soon be far less complex.

Once his bags were packed for the overseas journey, he drove to the saloon in Tombstone for a farewell drink. Pushing open the double doors, Zane bellied-up to the bar with a warm smile, quickly ordering a round of drinks for everyone.

His old coworkers were amazed to see the now famous conductor back in town and ran up to him excitedly. After all the handshaking and hugs, Zane started celebrating his last night in Tombstone by chugging on a bottle of Red Eye.

It had not been a good first day back at work for the deranged lawman. After the last gun battle of the day, Errol had settled in a booth in the far corner of the saloon, still wearing his bogus sheriff's attire

After laying low for weeks, he had just overheard the bar tender lamenting over the fact that Nella had been mortally wounded.

The unexpected and tragic news had felt like a hammer blow to his brain. When he questioned the barkeeper as to how it had happened, Errol was informed that she had been killed at a concert in Tucson several weeks back.

As he moped in his seat, dwelling despondently over the fact that the love of his life was gone forever, Franco Maximilian had somehow arisen from the grave and walked boldly into the tavern. Errol was completely flabbergasted.

He was certain that he had killed his hated rival at the Tucson concert, and couldn't quite grasp the fact that Franco was still alive and well. He watched all the attention the big shot conductor was receiving, getting more and more riled by the minute. When he had finally seen enough, he rose up from his hiding spot and walked up to Zane defiantly.

Wearing an angry scowl, he spewed, *"Well, look who we have here. Could it possibly be the one-armed idiot who jumped off a two-story roof without looking to see if his fall would be covered?"*

Zane was thrown off-guard at seeing his former rival. Not wanting any trouble on his last night in the states, Zane graciously offered Errol a beer.

"Let's let bygones be bygones, and drink to my new life," Zane toasted cheerfully.

Steaming with anger, Errol was having nothing to do with his avowed enemy's unwarranted success.

He stuck his face directly into Zane's, and sputtered, *"I'd rather die than drink with a lowlife like you! For starters, you soiled the reputation of my darling Nella. Then, you stole her away from me and dragged her to her untimely death. You are a despicable sidewinder, and I challenge you to a shootout at high noon tomorrow. I will avenge Nella's death by putting a hole between your beady little eyes!"*

Zane was dumbfounded by Errol's blatant challenge. As the crowd looked on in disbelief, he started to laugh nervously.

"Come on Errol, you know I had nothing to do with Nella's death. She was killed by an unknown assailant's bullet during my last concert. According to the news, some crazy old lady was trying to kill me, and Nella was unfortunately caught in the line of fire."

Errol scowled, replying, *"You really are a complete moron. For your information, I was the one who tried to kill you that night. I hid in the balcony, waiting to end your miserable life"*

Zane's mind started racing over the newspaper articles of the concert massacre. He quickly remembered the fact that that Nella had been shot in the back from a good distance. If the story was accurate, it must have been Errol's bullet that had tragically ended her life.

Bracing himself, Zane angrily informed Errol of his dire transgression.

"The paper reported that Nella was shot in the back. From your own admission, the only person to fire a gun from the balcony was you! With your illuminating confession, it now seems perfectly clear to me that you were the trigger-happy old lady in the balcony who killed Nella."

As Zane spoke, Errol replayed the chaotic concert scene in his mind, vaguely recalling a fancily dressed woman falling over the seat in front of her. With his voice starting to quiver, he questioned, *"Was Nella wearing a red dress?"*

Zane nodded his head gravely, and Errol let out a guttural moan.

When a fellow employee approached Errol to put a comforting arm around him, the ersatz sheriff angrily pushed him away. He quickly drew his personal revolver from its holster and planted it firmly in Zane's gut.

"I don't need anyone's pity. All I want is to see this devil die by my hand."

By that point, Zane had heard enough. Mustering all of his courage, he confronted the delusional Sherriff with the facts.

"Errol, you are a coldhearted murderer, and you deserve to be hung for killing Nella. I am going to get in my truck and drive to the police station. I will happily turn you in for the slaughter of all those innocent people. If you have any honor at all, you will accompany me to the precinct and confess to your crimes."

As he turned to leave the saloon, Errol swung his gun and cold cocked Zane from behind. As the man fell to the floor, Errol waved his revolver at the rest of the crowd, growling, *"Nobody's going anywhere. At high noon, we are all going into the street to watch me fill Franco Maximilian full of lead."*

Lesal Spurnell had been sitting impatiently in the doctor's office waiting for a consultation.

His boss had loaned him the money for much needed plastic surgery to remove the nasty scar that he had acquired during his Cuban prison stint. Lesal had never been a handsome man by any means, but the ill-fated facial disfigurement had transformed him into a roly-poly Frankenstein.

Growing more and more annoyed by the delay, he grabbed a magazine from the table and started randomly flipping through the pages. With his mind sifting over a dozen different things he needed to do, he threw the periodical down on the floor in disgust.

As the journal landed, the front page was exposed. Lesal looked down absently at the face on the cover and froze in disbelief. He quickly reached back down and grabbed the magazine. He scoured the picture for a few seconds and started to grin wildly. Without a doubt, it was definitely Zane Worth's face.

As he read the article carefully, he was confounded to learn that Zane had somehow transformed himself from a dimwitted counterfeiter and convicted criminal, to a one-armed Spanish orchestra conductor.

As preposterous as the situation seemed, Zane had not only evaded himself, along with the clueless Oklahoma law enforcement authorities, he was now the toast of musical society. Beyond belief, he had effectively hidden his illicit past from the world and had become rich and famous in the process.

Hanging on to the article, Lesal jumped out of his chair and hightailed it to his apartment. He packed his clothes and necessary equipment, then beelined it to the airport. As he settled into his first-class seat, he started writing down notes to organize and solidify a chase plan. For the first time in years, Lesal was an extremely happy man.

Once he arrived in Tucson, the gloating goon rented a car and drove to the symphony office.

The receptionist informed him that she hadn't seen the Maestro in weeks but passed on his home address. *"Even though Regina was killed months ago, I think her grieving lover may still be living there for free,"* the bitter secretary mentioned cynically.

Arriving at her residence, Lesal knocked on Regina's door, but there was no response. He waited for several minutes before deciding to search elsewhere. As he was about to drive off, he saw a gardener clipping the hedges.

He summoned the man over and asked if he knew where Franco might be. The caretaker shook his head no but did recall seeing him packing up the limo.

"The Maestro moved out quite a while ago. I think he mentioned coming here from some place south of Tucson, maybe Hereford or Ajo. Perhaps he's somewhere in that area."

Lesal gave the man an irritated look, then tossed him a twenty for the information. Just as he was pulling out of the driveway, the mob assassin saw the yard worker waving his hands frantically. He stopped and waited for the gardener to run-up to the window.

"I remember now. Mr. Maximilian told me that he had moved here from Tombstone."

Lesal arrived in the remote western community just after dark.

The downtown area seemed deserted except for some bright lights shining from the saloon. He parked a few blocks up the street and snuck-up to a side window. As he peered inside, he was stunned to see Zane standing motionless, with some yahoo lawman sticking a gun in his belly. When he overheard the heated exchange of words, and Errol's threat to gun Zane down at noon, he grinned from ear to ear.

Lesal was beside himself with joy. He had found his ever-elusive quarry, and the real fun was about to begin.

Sneaking back to his car, he hunted around the small town for a supply store. Stumbling across a hunting outfitter, he drove to the back. After jimmying open the lock, Lesal started his search for some necessary supplies.

He lifted a high-powered rifle, ammo, and some western duds. Now prepared to do battle, the conniving hitman drove back to the center of town.

He snuck up the backstairs to the saloon roof and took

a position where he had an unobstructed view of the street below. Finding a comfortable position against the railing, Lesal hunkered down and tilted his hat over his face. Just before he dozed off, he mumbled happily, *"My dear Mr. Worth, tomorrow is your day of reckoning."*

Errol had stayed up all night, keeping a wary eye on his hostages. Zane groggily awoke to find his wrists handcuffed to the bar. When his eyelids started fluttering, Errol walked over and threw a tankard of cold beer in his face to sober him up.

"Glad to see you're still alive. I didn't want you to miss all the fun of me blasting a hole in your forehead."

Zane's head felt like it was about to explode. Between the throbbing waves of pain, he started to remember the night's misfortunate sequence of events. Still hogtied to the bar, he plead, *"Errol, I know you really don't want to kill me. You're just distraught because you mistakenly killed Nella. You have to realize murdering me won't bring her back."*

Errol responded back bitterly, *"You have no idea of what I want; although seeing you squirm and beg for your life does cheer me up a tad. What will make me completely happy is to watch you falling backward to the dirt after my bullet has split your skull in half."*

As the sun neared its zenith, Errol ordered everyone out of the bar and on to the street.

"If anyone tries to interfere, or run for help, I will shoot them first. After I have gunned down Franco, you can do with me what you wish. Arrest or kill me, I really don't give a crap."

Dragging Zane to the infamous corral, Errol gave him a loaded pistol and commanded him to walk twenty paces.

As Zane and Errol slowly paced out the distance, a handful of curious tourists noticed the activity. Thinking that the mock gun battle reenactment was starting, they quickly joined the nervous locals lining the enclosure. When Zane counted the last step, he turned to face Errol.

Knowing that Franco was no match for his shooting skills, Errol shouted out arrogantly, *"To show you what a good sport I am, you can take the first shot."*

Zane slowly raised and pointed the pistol in Errol's direction. Sweating profusely, he was so nervous that he couldn't stop his hand from shaking. He had never been faced with having to deliberately kill another human being, and his conscience couldn't deal with the guilt. He just stood there, rooted firmly in his tracks.

When Errol realized that Franco was nothing but a yellowbellied coward, he screamed, *"I'm counting to ten. Then, I'm pulling the trigger, whether you're ready or not."*

As the Sherriff started his countdown, the Tombstone locals closed their eyes. They just could not bear to watch the impending bloodbath. On the count of ten, the blasting of guns were heard, along with the horror filled screams of the petrified townsfolk.

When the smoke cleared, only one man was left standing.

Miraculously, it was Zane, still shaking like a leaf in the wind. When the incredulous spectators saw Errol lying in a pool of his own blood, the crowd cheered wildly. They gathered around Zane in mass and started congratulating him with rowdy backslaps. The clueless tourists smiled in amusement, not realizing the gunplay had been for real.

One little boy dragged his mother to Errol's lifeless body and gave it a swift kick.

"See Mom, he really is dead!" His mother smiled amusedly,

replying, *"Yes Billy, isn't it just wonderful to see how realistic the show is! Now be careful, and don't get any of that fake blood on your shoes."*

As the pair wandered back to their car, the woman thought quizzically, *"I could be mistaken, but I though Wyatt Earp was supposed to be the good guy."*

After the sightseers had dispersed, the locals told Zane not to worry about the shooting. Since Errol had admitted to killing Nella and the other victims in Tucson, they had already agreed to cover Franco by saying that the incident had been an unfortunate accident. After fabricating a plausible story to the authorities, the one-armed hero was quickly cleared of any wrongdoing.

During the examination of Errol's fatal wound, the county corner scratched his head in confusion.

The cause of death was obvious, but the series of events leading up to his demise didn't seem to add up. If Errol had been shot by Franco, the bullet should have entered from the front of his head. Inexplicably, the bullet that caused Errol's fatal wound clearly had entered from the side.

As he mulled over the conundrum, he mumbled, *"Franco's bullet must have ricocheted off a wall and nailed him in the temple. That's what I call a lucky shot!"*

Worn out from his tedious day, and eager to break out the vodka bottle, the impatient coroner wrote the report and filed it away in a rush. If he had not been so distracted by the start of his happy hour, he could have easily deduced that the bullet that had ended Errol Cajo's skewed life hadn't come from Zane's gun.

CHAPTER 21
KILL THE WABBIT!

LESAL WAS CHOWING DOWN on a steak and egg breakfast at the local diner, beaming like a janitor who had just hit the lottery.

As he had planned, the shootout in Tombstone had been slightly rigged in Zane's favor. The mob assassin had hidden out on the saloon roof all night, waiting for the impending gun battle to begin. At the exact moment Errol shouted "*ten*", Lesal had shot him pointblank in the head with a single rifle shot.

There was no way in hell that Lesal was going to let some backwoods, dumb-ass Sheriff shoot his mark. No, Zane was his prize to snuff out, and he wanted to take some time to torture his victim properly before he wasted him. Mr. Worth had earned months of agonizing retribution, and Lesal was going to enjoy every single second of it.

Getting into his rental car, he found a place to park near Zane's trailer that was well hidden from view. Turning off the motor, he waited to see what his prey's next move would be.

Zane loaded his bags into the bed of his old pickup and started his journey to Sky Harbor International Airport in Phoenix. His first destination was Paris, where he was engaged to conduct a week's worth of concerts. With his mind focused solely on his new adventures, he failed to notice a car trailing him.

As Lesal tailed Zane, he was smiling like the Cheshire cat. He had waited a very long time for this moment, and the renewed chase had left him entirely euphoric.

Recalling his favorite cartoon character, Elmer Fudd, the stubby mobster jokingly mocked, *"You better watch out Mr. Worth, its wabbit hunting season!"*

CHAPTER 22
CAT AND MOUSE GAMES

AFTER A TWELVE-HOUR FLIGHT, Zane had settled into his hotel room overlooking Les Champs Elysees.

As he looked out at the Arc de Triomphe in the distance, he marveled at the cosmopolitan flair and ornate architecture of the ancient European city. Ready to take on the finest orchestras in the Old World, Zane opened his laptop and started viewing videos of the musical works on his upcoming concerts.

The first few practices with the Parisian orchestra had gone quite well, considering Zane spoke absolutely no French. This morning's dress rehearsal was his last chance to polish the intricate details of the musical score. By adding a few nuances here and there, he was sure that his first concert at the Salle Pleyel would be a spectacular success.

The musicians of the Orchestre de Paris had been unusually quiet, yet cordial, so Zane couldn't be sure if they respected his conducting or were just being gracious.

Unlike his former ensemble, all the French musicians played with exceptional skill and aplomb. He finished the last few pages in the score and ended the rehearsal session early, with the musicians applauding him politely.

Zane's heart swelled with pride, knowing that the evening's concert was going to be the best performance of his life.

At 8PM sharp, the concertmaster walked on stage and the cued the oboist to tune the ensemble. Zane followed, strutting confidentially to the podium. One could hear a pin drop as the Maestro raised his arm to get the musician's attention.

As he prepared to give his opening downbeat, he looked down at his music in horror.

Scribbled over the first page of his score was the message, *"Bonjour, you stupid pinhead, I'm Bach."* Under the poorly punned script was an unhappy face with its tongue poking out.

Zane let out an involuntary yelp, and a collective gasp from the orchestra and audience alike was heard rumbling through the hall.

Trying to gather his wits, Zane started the overture with jerky arm gestures. As the music progressed, all Zane could think about was the fact that Lesal Spurnell had caught up with him. He wondered if the thug was out in the hall, taking aim at him this very second. The terrifying mental image panicked him, and he started to conduct erratically.

Ignoring his abrupt changes in tempo, Zane ducked and darted around spasmodically, trying to dodge any bullets that Lesal may try to fire at him.

In short order, the music had reached breakneck speed, with the musicians trying valiantly to keep up Zane's flailing arm. The overture ended with a flurry of exaggerated gestures from the exhausted musicians and frantic conductor.

With his brain reeling with fear, Zane collapsed onto his music stand.

Instantly, the crowd went wild with applause. Somewhat surprised by the audience's response, Zane turned to make an abrupt bow, then leapt offstage as though his very life depended on it.

Lesal had been sitting in the balcony watching the whole frenzied affair. By the end of the first piece, he had started laughing uncontrollably, seeing how visibly terrified his prey had become after reading his calling card.

Getting up to exit the hall, he mused, *"This is just the beginning of my fun. By the time I'm finished, you'll be begging me to end your miserable life."*

When the impresario signaled for Zane to return to the podium for the second half of the show, the obstinate conductor refused. There was nothing on Earth that could get him back in Lesal's crosshairs.

To Zane's dismay, the no-nonsense French manager wasn't taking no for an answer. He grabbed the conductor by the belt and pitched him unceremoniously onto the stage. Trying to regain his composure, Zane accidentally tripped over his feet as he mounted the podium. The quick-thinking concertmaster caught him by the arm, then helped steady him.

Zane tried to open the score, but his hand was shaking uncontrollably. He could feel Lesal hot breath on the back of his neck and was certain he was a goner.

As he prepared to give the downbeat, Zane had an epiphany.

With the assassin hiding somewhere in the hall, he was certain that he would be dead by the symphony's end. If this concert was going to be his final hurrah, Zane was going to go out with unabashed panache. Taking a deep breath, he started the same Beethoven symphony that he had conducted on his debut concert in Tucson.

Bit by bit, his jumpy arm movements calmed, and he started conducting with conviction. Keeping his eyes closed, he caressed each musical phrase with passion. His heartfelt expressions moved the musicians to new heights of musical ecstasy, and the sounds the ensemble produced were simply magnificent.

When the fifth symphony ended with its monumental final chords, the crowd flew to their feet, clapping and shouting their accolades for the soulful Spanish Maestro.

Zane bowed reverently, then quickly exited. When the crowd wouldn't stop applauding, the insistent stage manager shoved him back, his stern look letting Zane know to stay put until the audience was through with their ovation.

Returning to his dressing room, Zane collapsed into an overstuffed chair. All he could think about was Lesal, and why the goon hadn't killed him during the concert.

Trapped in an inescapable quandary, he wasn't sure which way to turn next.

If he fled now, he knew he would quickly run out of money. Without cold hard cash, it would be impossible for him to hideout in a life style that he felt he deserved.

Thankfully, he had five upcoming concert engagements. If he was able to survive that long, Zane was sure he would have the resources needed to escape from Lesal Spurnell's grasp permanently. Admitting to the fact that he really didn't have a choice in the matter, he pulled on his overcoat and walked nervously into the chilly November air.

In Berlin, Lesal kept up his diabolical torments, positive that his prey would be kept in a constant state of panic.

After Zane had left his hotel for a morning rehearsal, Lesal had snuck up to his hotel room, deftly using a skeleton key to unlock the door. He dipped his finger into some Vaseline and traced an invisible calling card onto the bathroom mirror.

When Zane emerged from his shower the next morning, there was a huge scowling face, angrily staring at him through the fogged glass.

Wondering if Lesal was still hiding close by, Zane turned white as a sheet.

His stomach started grinding with stabbing pain, and he was instantly covered in cold sweat. Throwing a towel around his waist, he ran into the living area looking for the mobster. Relieved to find no sign of Mr. Spurnell, Zane collapsed on the bed.

The ache in his solar plexus was unbearable and he felt like he was going to pass out from the pain. With a depressing wave of angst washing over his body, he muttered, *"I can't take much more of this. When is this fiendish mind game going to end?"*

Lesal carefully bided his time, knowing that Zane could not evade his ever- watchful surveillance. Using his knack for disguises, the mobster had gotten within an arm's length of his target many times.

After following Zane to a restaurant, he had bribed the greedy maître d' so he could wait on Zane's table. Dressed in a tuxedo, he had disguised himself with a scraggily hair piece and thick bushy beard.

After bowing respectfully, Lesal put on a phony German accent.

"Vat vould you like to order, mine heir?" he croaked. With his mind totally distracted by the sadistic huntsman, Zane quickly replied, *"Whatever you think is best on the menu."*

Lesal bowed once more and headed to the kitchen.

As the pudgy hoodlum waddled away, Zane playfully mused, *"From the looks of my waiter, the food must be really good here."*

The assassin soon returned with Zane's meal and placed it ceremoniously on the table.

"Is zer any zing else I can bring you?" Zane smiled weakly and shook his head no.

After Lesal had withdrawn, Zane grabbed his napkin and placed it over his lap. The aroma of the food had made him ravenously hungry and he grabbed for his fork.

When he looked down into his plate, Zane's face flushed. The traditional German fare of Brats and sauerkraut had been laid out most peculiarly.

The pickled cabbage was spread in a circle over the dish, with two boiled potatoes looking much like eyes. The sausages were placed in an upside-down U at the bottom; purposely making the finished dish look like an edible scowling face.

Zane turned around in a flash, looking for the rotund server, but he had already disappeared into the kitchen.

Realizing that Lesal had been just a few inches away from him, Zane had a nervous breakdown. Like an ambushed Gazelle, he sprung up from his chair in utter panic. Leaping around the other patron's tables like a pride of lions were in pursuit, Zane raced out of the restaurant, howling like a banshee.

Lesal watched the frenetic escape scene from the kitchen door, laughing until he almost choked. *"I've never felt this alive in my entire life,"* the fiend spewed. *"Unfortunately, I will have to end this game soon."*

"Mr. Worth, you'd better enjoy your highfalutin career while you can!"

CHAPTER 23
NEW YEAR'S EVE FINALE

AGAINST ALL ODDS, ZANE had survived to the end of his tour.

His final engagement was directing the Vienna Philharmonic for their New Year's Gala. Conducting this highly coveted event was the dream of every famous music director, and Zane's reputation for delivering electrifying concerts had easily landed him the job.

For the past few weeks, Mr. Spurnell seemed to have vanished. Since the ever-present predator had left none of his unsettling calling cards, Zane started to wonder if he had given up the chase. Perhaps Lesal's mob boss had called the gangster back to the States. After musing over another option, Zane secretly hoped that another assassin had finally gunned Lesal down.

In any event, once he collected his last fee, he would have over a million euros. Without question, Zane knew that his newfound wealth would be more than enough to effectively evade Lesal Spurnell forever.

Through no fault of his own, Lesal had been momentarily distracted from his heavenly crusade. When Axel discovered that his repulsive assassin had been roaming about Europe, the mob boss had ordered his underling to settle an unpaid debt.

The target was a delinquent Duke with a predilection for gambling. After amassing a fortune in losses, the unlucky blueblood had taken out a large loan from the casino. When the Duke's losing streak continued, the gaming establishment insisted that he write a bank draft for the several million euros he owed.

Having no intention of paying back the money, the royal rat quickly fled to his estate in Estonia. He had been hiding there ever since, protected behind the massive stone walls of his 17th century fortress.

Wanting to demonstrate to future slackers the consequences of not paying back their cash advances, the irate casino owner had hired the services of Lesal's mob to execute the deadbeat Duke.

It had taken a bit of trickery to enter the estate, but Mr. Spurnell had finally managed to gain entrance by hitching a ride in a laundry truck.

Hiding in a hamper, the duke's staff had carelessly lugged Lesal to the linen room, amazed at the weight of the container. When the guard's curiosity finally got the best of them, they open the bin to see what could be making it so cumbersome. Much to their surprise, Lesal sprang out and shot them both pointblank.

After a brief search, Lesal discovered his mark sitting in front of a huge flat screen TV, talking on the phone with a bookie. *"Ten-thousand on the Red Skin's to lose,"* the man barked, ending the call with an annoyed sigh.

Without making a sound, the creepy hooligan snuck up behind the Duke, then coldcocked him across the back of his head.

When the royal louse came to, he found his body bound tightly to a chair. To his surprise, he discovered that one of his arms was left free. Sitting across the table was Lesal Spurnell, pointing a gun at his nose.

"What in hell is going on here?" the Duke questioned arrogantly.

"Apparently, you don't seem to want to honor your gambling debts," the assassin quipped back. Grinning maliciously, Lesal slowly pulled a pair of dice from his coat pocket.

"Since you seem to enjoy gaming so much, I'll going to make you a deal. If you roll any number other than a seven or eleven, I will let you live. If a seven or eleven comes up, I will put a bullet into your worthless body. I call the game craps with a painful twist."

Lesal placed the dice in front of the Duke's free arm and sat back with a sneer.

"Imbecile! You simply cannot go around shooting royalty! You don't seem to understand that I am a very important man! And what if I refuse?"

Lesal responded back curtly, *"I don't care if you're the fricken Pope. I'll happily blow your brains out before you take your next breath. Roll now or die where you sit. I just thought you might want a sporting chance, but it's your call."*

The Duke grabbed the dice hesitantly, his hand visibly trembling.

Inhaling shakily, he threw the dice, pleading, *"For the love of God, don't let a seven or eleven come up."* After his throw, he stared at the spinning cubes with a look of impending catastrophe.

"Seven," Lesal called out amusedly.

Taking careful aim, he fired the weapon. The bullet pierced the Duke's bound arm, and the man screamed in agony.

"That was some bad luck there, Dukie. I bet that arm hurts!"

Since I'm such a nice guy, I am going to give you another chance to live, so roll the dice again. If any other number besides the 7/11 combo comes up, I will walk out the door."

Grimacing with pain, the duke scooped up the dice. Blowing on them, he begged, *"Lady Luck, please don't let me down. My life depends on your merciful kindness."* Giving the dice a toss, he closed his eyes tightly and prayed for his souls salvation.

"Eleven. So sorry, but you lose again."

This time Lesal shot his victim in the left knee, commenting callously, *"It seems clear to me that neither God, nor Lady Luck give a holy crap for you."*

As his victim writhed in anguish, Lesal cheerily offered, *"I'm feeling unusually generous today, so I'm going to give you one more chance. You are already painfully aware the rules and I think it's highly appropriate that your compulsion should determine your destiny."*

Blowing on the capricious cubes for luck, the Duke tossed the dice. He watched the spinning squares in horror, frantic to avoid seeing the two dreaded numbers.

The first die quickly stopped on a one, while the other seemed to spin on its axis for an eternity. As the second whirling die finally dropped to its side, a six was revealed.

"Funny, but I always thought seven was a lucky number," Lesal chuckled tauntingly.

No longer amused by his cruel torment, the mobster's face instantly morphed into a scowl. *"In your case, it was your death roll."*

Without a moment's hesitation, Lesal aimed the Glock at the Duke's chest and fired. He watched his victim fall backward to the floor, then slowly bleed out over a priceless Persian rug. Wearing a contemptuous sneer, Lesal pried open the dead man's mouth with his fingers and shoved the dice inside.

Wiping the Duke's spittle off his hand, the sadistic brute commented smugly, *"I always knew those loaded dice would come in handy one day."*

Lesal stepped into the bitterly cold winter air feeling completely renewed. *"That was a nice warm up for the main event,"* he mused. *"Now, it's time to finish my quest, Zane Worth. Ready or not, you're about to meet your maker!"*

The Viennese New Year's fest was about to begin. The concert hall had been set with numerous tables so the audience members could indulge in food and drink during the show.

The orchestra members had already taken their places, and the crowd was anxiously awaiting the entrance of the infamous Maestro Franco Maximilian.

Dressed in his white tie and tails, Zane walked to the podium exuding confidence. There was an immediate hush in the audience as the one-armed conductor took his place. When the lights dimmed, he tapped his music stand to get the orchestra's attention.

Just as he about to give the opening downbeat, a sharp pop rang out.

An inattentive waiter had opened a bottle of champagne and the sound reverberated through the hall like a cannon shot. Like a heatseeking missile, the cork flew from the bottle and hit Zane squarely in the back of the head.

Thinking Lesal Spurnell had just taken a potshot at him, Zane leapt from the podium into the viola section, landing on top of three very surprised musicians.

Assuming that this was another one of the Maestro's crazy antics, the audience started cheering and clapping wildly.

Once he realized he was unharmed, Zane dusted himself off and remounted the podium. Before starting the first *Strauss* Waltz, he turned to the audience and bowed graciously. With the audience and musicians staring at him intently, he began the concert.

The musical gala proceeded with Zane giving the best show of his career. Flailing and gyrating exuberantly, the normally dour orchestra musicians quickly followed his lead. They played with unusual gusto and élan, and the audience flew to their feet at the concert's finale. Zane received three rowdy standing ovations from the overjoyed and somewhat inebriated crowd.

Back in his dressing room, Zane pocketed his paycheck, and broke open his own bottle of bubbly in celebration of his final concert. As he toasted to himself, he started to read the cards attached to the numerous bouquets of flowers lining his dressing room.

Hidden behind the hedges of roses and baby's-breath, was a nondescript vase containing a single wilted carnation. Somewhat surprised at the pitiful offering, Zane grabbed the card and opened it. Inside was an unhappy face with a scribbled warning, *"I hope you enjoyed your last performance, moron. You'll be dead before morning!"*

Without missing a beat, Zane turned and raced out of the building in a flash.

He hailed a cab and hollered, *"Airport, and step on it!"*

CHAPTER 24
TROUBLE AT TWENTY
THOUSAND FEET

ARRIVING AT THE DEPARTURE gate, Zane checked in to confirm his one-way, first class ticket to Bangkok. With everything in order, he realized he needed to visit the restroom before boarding.

Moments later, Lesal walked to the ticket counter and purchased a ticket on the same flight. Being a master of disguise, the assassin had dressed as an Arab business man. Along with his flowing robe and traditional Kaffiyeh, Lesal had donned a scraggily beard and dark aviator sun glasses.

Hearing the first-class boarding announcement over the intercom, Zane hurried onto the aircraft.

Settled in his seat, he watched the rest of the passengers enter, checking out each person carefully to make sure Lesal Spurnell wasn't slipping on. When the outer door was shut and locked, Zane let out a sigh of relief. Satisfied that he had ditched the tenacious mobster, Zane asked the flight attendant for a single malt scotch on the rocks.

As the jet taxied down the tarmac, Zane kicked back and took a sip of his drink. The roar of the jet turbines slowly started to comfort the jumpy fugitive and he slowly nodded off, knowing that he had evaded his archenemy.

Some moderate air turbulence awoke Zane, and he jerked up with a start.

After a prolonged stretch of his arms and legs, he reached for his scotch. Downing the rest of the drink, he went to set the empty glass back. To his astonishment, a frowning face had been traced on the paper coaster.

Zane instantly felt like he was about to throw up. Peeking timidly around his seat, he surveyed the rest of the cabin looking for Lesal Spurnell. From what he could see, most of the passengers seem to be napping or engaged in some sort of reading material.

His gaze finally rested on a Middle Eastern man in mid-cabin. Something about him seemed to be slightly awry. With his head gear and dark glasses, his face was totally obscured. Zane decided to check him out a bit more closely and rose from his seat to use the bathroom.

As he walked by, he glanced down furtively. The mysterious foreigner was reading a financial publication and seemed completely engrossed and unaware of Zane's passing. Feeling slightly relieved, Zane open the door of the lavatory and started to enter.

Out of the corner of his eye, he saw the Arab man turn completely around and stare intently in his direction. Slamming the door shut, Zane sat on the toilet, his brain reeling with fear.

As he contemplated his next move, there was a knock at the door.

Zane flushed the commode and called out, *"Just a minute."* When he stepped out the door, he nearly ran into the mysterious stranger.

Zane quickly sidestepped around the man and hurried back to his seat.

Starting to shake uncontrollably, he was sure that the robe clad man was the despised mobster. Although he couldn't see the Arab's face, Zane was already well aware of Lesal's knack for disguises. Having an inspired thought, Zane pushed the call button for the flight attendant. When she appeared, Zane motioned for her to lean over.

He whispered urgently, *"I saw a Muslim man praying in the coach section. From the tone of his voice, he seemed to be quite agitated about something. When he was finished, he grabbed a package from under his seat and moved quickly toward the restroom. The whole affair seemed highly suspicious, and in this age of terrorism, you cannot be too careful."*

The attendant gasped, her cheeks immediately flushing with blood. She scurried to the intercom and called out a numbered code. The rest of the crew quickly dropped what they were doing and huddled together, deep in heated discussion.

Testing out his disguise, Lesal had followed Zane to the back of the plane. When his prey had not reacted, the Arab garbed goon had entered the lavatory.

Once settled on the toilet bowl, Lesal discovered that he was experiencing an unexpected bout of diarrhea. Without any reading material to entertain him, the tone-deaf hoodlum started singing his favorite song. Unfortunately for Mr. Spurnell, the atonal blathering sounded much like Muslim call to prayer.

After hearing the man's raspy sounding adhan, the flight crew panicked and surrounded the door.

Lesal was now experiencing intense gastro-intestinal problems and was nowhere near ready to vacate the safety of the cubical when he heard a rap on the door.

"Sir, you need to come out of the lavatory right this minute!"

Lesal was not the least bit amused by the intrusion. *"I'm taking an unholy crap, so leave me the hell alone,"* he shouted at the top of his lungs.

An undercover Federal Air Marshal had been watching the scene at the back of the aircraft intently.

He had boarded the flight after receiving a tip from homeland security. The agent had reported on a suspicious looking foreign passenger booking a one-way ticket. Although his credentials had checked out, the suspect had seemed nervous and unnecessarily abrasive.

After checking his gun, the officer exited his seat in a flash and joined the bevy of flight attendants at the bathroom door. After rapping loudly, he yelled, *"I'm a Federal Air Marshall. I order you to vacate this lavatory immediately."*

Not even close to finishing his business, the mobster angrily kicked at the door with his foot and spewed, *"I don't give a damn who you are. You can kiss my volcanic ass!"*

Hearing Lesal's defiant retort, the lawman took a step back and bashed in the door with his shoulder.

Taken by surprise, Lesal grabbed hold of his robe in a futile attempt to retain his dignity. The Marshall drew back his fist, punching Lesal squarely in the jaw and the alleged terrorist fanatic was knocked unconscious.

Zane watched the entire chaotic scene with an evil smirk on his face. When he saw the pintsized porker securely handcuffed, and still out cold in the back of the plane, he pushed the service button.

When the flustered flight attendant arrived, he ordered, *"Another scotch please, and make it a double."*

When the jet landed in Bangkok, Zane looked on as a handful of Thai security officers led Lesal off the jet.

Cursing and struggling violently, the hood glared at Zane and raved, *"When I get out of this, I will hunt you down. Once you're in my grasp, I will torture you for months. When you have been mercilessly abused and are begging me to end your life, I will make you suffer even more. When I've had my well-deserved satisfaction, I will choke you with my bare hands and watch you slowly expire. I will not stop until I have squeezed the last breath out of your worthless body!"*

"No matter where you run, there is no place on earth that you can hide from me. I swear to God, I will find you and when I do, you're a dead ..." By that time, the Air Marshall had heard enough and punched Lesal soundly in the gut to shut him up.

Feigning confusion, Zane snapped back angrily, *"I hope you like Thai food, you crazy terrorist."*

CHAPTER 25
THREE BEST FRIENDS REUNITE

IN A POOL ATOP a five-star Bangkok Hotel, Zane floated lazily while basking in the early morning sun. He gazed past the pools edge to the lush greenery below and smiled contently. For the first time in years, he felt totally unencumbered.

To his delight, the English morning news edition had featured the capture of a murderous mobster, named Lesal Spurnell.

The homicidal hoodlum was wanted in twenty different countries for his heinous crimes, and the United States was demanding his extradition to face charges ranging from racketeering and extortion, to assignation. After finishing the article, Zane was absolutely positive that Lesal would be locked behind bars for several lifetimes.

As he mused over his good fortune, Zane realized how much he enjoyed the tropical setting of Thailand. As the warm sultry breezes wafted over him, his nostrils caught the intoxicating fragrance of plumeria and jasmine flowers, intermixed with a hint of rotting mangos.

The unique aroma brought back nostalgic memories of Puerto

Vallarta, and Zane had an inspired idea. Snapped his fingers, he requested one of the waiters to bring him the house phone. After a brief conversation, he hung up the receiver and ordered a cocktail.

After a few restful weeks at the posh Thai resort, Zane boarded a jet bound for Mexico. He had realized that the best time of his life had been spent with his prison buddies back in Puerto Vallarta.

Late the next evening, Zane walked up the stairs to the rooftop bar of the Blue Chairs Hotel. Sitting at a table by the outer railing were both his buddies, downing Corona's in typical fashion.

When he approached the pair, they looked up and gasped as though they had seen a ghost. Once the men realized it was Zane in the flesh, they jumped up from the table and ran to their best friend. After hugs all-around, they all sat at the table with Lumpy and Slim spewing out a million questions.

Zane laughed heartily, telling them to slow down a bit. He reassured them that they had the rest of their lives to catch-up on his many adventures.

"Just one question," said Slim with a troubled look. *"What in hell happened to your arm?"* Zane grabbed a beer, then told the story of his unfortunate accident in Tombstone.

"Jeez," Lumpy swore. *"Did you get that asshole back?"*

Zane's face hardened after reflecting back upon the tragic news of Errol shooting Nella. Unlike his gang leaders accidental death, Zane had felt no remorse after thinking he had killed Errol.

"Don't worry, my friend. He got exactly what was coming to him," Zane responded coldly.

After taking a deep breath, he raised up his beer. Inviting his friends to a toast, Zane shouted, *"Here's to our reunion and the good life!"* They all clanked their bottles together and swore, *"To undying friendship, now and forever!"*

After a few months of living at the Blue Chairs Hotel, Zane grew weary of the daily chaos and frenzied partying of the guests. Although he was most fond of his gay brethren, he decided to buy a bungalow a mile south of the city to get some peace and quiet.

Nestled on the mountain side, and surrounded by lush jungle, the house fit his requirements to a tee. With a secluded beach was just a few hundred yards down the mountain, it was a peaceful and safe retreat from the rest of the world.

Wanting his two closest friends nearby, Zane insisted on moving Slim and Lumpy in with him. The pair found the isolated setting calming, but soon realized that they missed all the hubbub and interaction of life in the city. After bringing up their concerns, Zane thought it might be fun to open a bar and grill on the beach.

Two months later, the *"Tres Desperados"* beach cantina opened for business.

Water taxis brought customers in from town, and a dock provided space for those with their own boats. Lumpy managed the grill while Slim ran the bar. Zane took on the role of host since he enjoyed schmoozing with the customers. Once the word had spread, the beach bar became a very popular destination for tourists and locals alike.

All three men found the enterprise highly rewarding, and their lives quickly became far more productive and entertaining.

One late night, after the last customer had departed the bar, Zane requested an unexpected toast. With all three men's drinks in the air, Zane cracked an amused sneer.

"Let's raise our glasses to Lesal Spurnell. If it were not for his unrelenting pursuit, I would have never met my two best friends in the world. May the dirty, rotten, fat bastard fester in prison for the rest of his miserable existence!"

CHAPTER 26
BANGKOK BUST OUT

LESAL HAD BEEN LOCKED behind the bars of countless prisons in the past, but never in such a squalid and ruthless penitentiary.

The day he was incarcerated, the guards threw him in a holding cell with fifty other Thai felons. Each of the inmates took a turn poking his potbelly, and then laughing hysterically. With each disrespectful jab, the goon became more incensed.

Finally losing his temper, he grabbed a very surprised prisoner by the neck and bit off a good part of his nose. As he stood ground, defiantly chewing on the poor man's proboscis, he growled, *"Anyone else want to touch me?"* The horrified inmates quickly huddled in the far corner, glaring in revulsion at the cannibalistic ogre.

While the US Federal Attorneys and Thai officials took their time negotiating Lesal Spurnell's extradition terms, the heinous hitman terrorized the inmate population. Each day, he picked a new victim to torture, taking his frustrations out in a variety of perverse and aberrant ways.

Astounded by the stubby gangsters ferocity, the prison warden wisely moved him to solitary confinement after Lesal had filled the infirmary to overflowing with severely maimed patients.

Thai mob informants had passed on intel to Axel Gilan that his mini mobster was being flown back to New York City to face trial in the next few weeks. To say the least, the boss was not at all pleased by the news.

Lesal knew enough about the syndicate to have the entire organization locked up for life. Not willing to take the chance that Mr. Spurnell might spill the beans in return for special treatment from the Fed's, Axel made plans to break the gruesome goon out of his Thai pen before he could be shipped back to the States.

It was an uneventful Sunday afternoon, and the majority of Thai prisoners were outdoors in the exercise area. Lesal was locked up in his private cell since he didn't seem to mingle well with the rest of the inmates.

Axel and five cohorts boldly entered the prison and asked to see the Warden. Within minutes, the unsuspecting administrator walked into the room and was immediately accosted along with the rest of the guards inside.

Pointing his gun at the man's head, the Axel demanded Lesal's immediate release. When the blubbering Warden hesitated, the impatient thug put a bullet in his brain. With the Warden's keys in hand, Gilan's gang capped the rest of the guards, and then went on the hunt for Lesal.

The mobster was first shocked, then overjoyed to see his boss opening his cell door. When he was freed, the hideous hitman got on his hands and knees and started kissing his rescuers feet. With a moan of disgust, Axel told him to snap out of it and get up. With his men in tow, the mob boss barked out orders to head for the prison yard.

Knowing that they would need some additional chaos to aid in their escape, the gangsters shot the few remaining guards patrolling the yard. While the stunned inmates looked on in confusion, Axel's men unpinned several hand grenades and blew open the front gate.

The mêlée that followed was exactly what Mr. Gilan needed to mask the mob's departure. With the inmates fleeing helter-skelter to freedom, the gang loaded into their vehicle and sped away undetected.

Twenty minutes later, they had boarded the syndicates private jet and were flying back to Brooklyn.

If Axel Gilan had any inkling of the future problems Lesal would cause, he would have shot his smarmy subordinate between his close-set eyes and let the voracious prison rats dine on his corpulent carcass.

Understanding the urgency for Lesal to lay low and out of sight, Axel Gilan sequestered him to a dingy apartment in a rundown tenement in Yonkers.

With a mob guard posted outside the door 24 hours a day, absolutely no one was allowed in or out. Lesal's food and fresh clothing were passed through a metal hatch, and the only door to his room was barred and locked securely.

For the first few months Lesal resigned himself to his fate. He appreciated the fact that his gang had gone to such extreme lengths to rescue him, but being locked away in a shabby, six-by-eight room made it feel like he had never left his Thailand cell.

Just as he had given up hope of ever seeing the outside world again, he was given a fortuitous break.

While passing Lesal's food to him through the opening

in the door, the inattentive guard had accidentally left his cell phone on the tray under a napkin. As the porky con started to devour his dinner, he noticed the devise and almost gagged on his cheeseburger. Moving to the far corner to the room, he punched in the number of the one man who could help him.

Rudge Wilik was a fellow gangster who owed Lesal a big favor.

Nicknamed *"Rudge the Grudge"* by the mob for his insatiable craving for retribution, the ill-fated gangster had been captured by a rival syndicate member several years back.

Just as Rudge was about to be executed by the goon, Lesal Spurnell appeared out of thin air and had wasted the unsuspecting ambusher before he could finish his task, thus saving Mr. Wilik's life.

After listening to Lesal's hushed request, Rudge knew it was time to repay the favor.

A few hours later, *the Grudge* arrived at the apartment building with a box of doughnuts. He trudged up the stairs to the fifth floor and walked up to the thug protecting Lesal's room. Telling the guard the crullers were a gift from the big boss, Rudge handed the package over.

First checking the box for any contraband, the guard rapped loudly on the door. When Lesal didn't answer, the man shouted, *"Hey Spurnell! Da' boss got yo fat ass some Krispy Kreme's."* Hearing no response, the curious guard opened the latch to peered inside.

As he bent over, Rudge lunged down, shoving the man's head through the opening, holding him there determinedly.

Hiding next to the pass-through, Lesal swiftly grabbed the guards head and gave it a violent twist. After hearing the sickly sound of cracking vertebrae, Lesal pushed the dead man's head back through the opening. His accomplice located the guard's keys and let Lesal out.

Before he departed, Lesal turned to Rudge with an amused grin. *"Thanks pallie, now were even."*

After a hearty handshake, the freed mob assassin quickly exited the building and caught a cab to his apartment to gather the items he would need to resume his passionate pursuit.

While packing his outfits, the hefty hood realized the irony of the situation he was facing. He was certain that Axel would not be pleased with his escape and would place a substantial price on his head to keep him quiet permanently. While on the hunt for Zane, Lesal knew he was going to be pursued after by every gangster looking to make some quick cash.

With a tinge of arrogance, the goon assumed that the reward would be a half-million dollars or more. He knew that kind of moolah would bring a lot of money hungry cockroaches out of the woodwork. Above all else, Lesal knew he would have to be extremely wary. Any slipup on his part would turn out to be a deadly mistake. To evade detection by the highly motivated bounty hunters, Lesal knew without a doubt that he needed to rely on his camouflage expertise.

The first item on his agenda was to locate his quarry quickly. Lesal realized he had spent more than eight months in confinement. With that kind of head start and plenty of cash to throw around, Zane Worth could be hiding out pretty much anywhere on the planet.

After entering the airport terminal, the blubbery beast headed for the ladies' bathroom. After scoping out the door for a few seconds, he ran in and locked himself inside a stall. Five minutes later, a bleach-blonde and entirely bizarre looking shemale walked out the lavatory door wearing a flowery tent of a dress. After hiking up his bulky bodice, he sashayed confidently to the ticket counter.

A disgruntled female airline agent asked how she could help

him. Without trying to disguise his voice, he barked, *"I want a ticket to Mexico City,"*

The unavoidable look on the woman's face conveyed both her surprise and amusement. Before she had a chance to respond, Lesal continued, *"I'm heading to a cross dressers convention in the Zona Rosa. You have a problem with that?"*

Trying her best not to burst out laughing, she quickly typed in the information.

"Miss Spurnell, would you like first class or coach?"

The mobster pulled out a pile of cash, responding back arrogantly, *"What do you think doll face?"* After entering more data on the computer, she looked up hesitantly and asked with veiled smirk, *"One seat or two?"*

"Don't get funny with me you boll-legged baboon! Just give my fricken boarding pass," Lesal growled threateningly.

After seeing the peeved look in his eye, the impertinent agent finished her typing and handed the hoodlum his travel documents and identification. As he turned toward his departure gate, the woman cooed out loudly, *"Have a nice flight... Madam!"*

Not wanting to attract undo attention, Lesal kept moving while sputtering under his breath, *"If I ever see that snotty sow again, I'll rip her throat out!"*

During the eight-hour transit, Lesal endured never-ending looks of shock and sporadic snickering from his fellow passengers. Already apprised of the hideous abomination sitting in first class, the gossipy flight crew had spread the word like wildfire. The open mockery infuriated him to no end, but Lesal managed to remain calm. He knew he couldn't take the chance of being arrested by airport security again.

In Mexico City, he hailed a cab and ordered, *"Take me to a top-notch Hotel and make it snappy!"* The cabbie nodded and quickly pulled into a sea of cars.

After being stuck in nightmarish traffic for hours, the taxi pulled up to a classy high-rise building. Lesal jumped out, throwing twenty bucks on the front seat. The cabbie protested and held his hand out signaling that he wanted more cash.

Tossing him a fifty, Lesal moaned, *"Jesus Christ! Everybody's a crook these days."*

After paying off the driver he grabbed his suitcase and walked enticingly to the front desk. *"I want your best suite,"* the horrendously dressed hitman demanded. Without missing a beat, the concierge rang for a bellhop to take his bag, and replied, *"Have a wonderful stay here in Mexico!"*

Lesal scoffed and replied, *"I'd rather be trapped in Detroit for the rest of my life then be stuck in this miserable excuse for a country for an hour."*

Once Lesal's elevator door had closed, the front desk man shook his head slowly. He then mumbled with a sigh, *"Dios Mio! That was the ugliest woman I have ever seen in my life."*

When Lesal's boss discovered that his cagey convict had flown the coop, he was immediately incensed. Once Axel had thought through all the ramifications of Lesal's escape, he turned white as a sheet.

In a panic, he quickly called an emergency meeting of all the East Coast syndicate leaders. Axel knew if Lesal was ever captured by the Feds, his testimony would bring down all of the Northeast crime organizations.

Relaying the facts to his fellow mob counterparts, a contract was immediately put out on the escapee's head. The five crime moguls each put in two-hundred-thousand dollars, to be paid in full to the man who took down Lesal Spurnell.

As the word spread, every hitman on the east coast started hunting for the squat, million-dollar payday.

When Alex Gilan awoke the next morning, he was confounded by the fact that each and every one of his men had disappeared into thin air. Once he realized his entire gang was scouring the metropolis looking for Mr. Spurnell, he shook his head in resignation, knowing that business was going to be very slow for the time being.

Three days later, Axel Gilan was at his wit's end.

In their fevered pursuit to collect the exorbitant bounty, trigger-happy hoods were shooting every short, overweight man that looked remotely like Lesal Spurnell. In New York City alone, over twenty ill-fated men had already been gunned down.

The ever-vigilant NYPD had gone on high alert, and there was abject panic on the streets. Terrified to walk outside after dark, the majority of the citizenry had locked themselves inside their homes and the Big Apple had come to a standstill.

When the police caught wind of the big money hit, they started rounding up mobsters by the dozens. Soon, most all of the criminal element from Brooklyn to Philadelphia was cooped up in jail awaiting murder charges.

By the end of the week Axel Gilan was finally fed up. Grabbing his coat and sidearm, the man strode out the door muttering, *"I guess I'll have to take care of that overstuffed little son of a bitch myself!"*

⋙⋘

After hiding out in his Mexico City suite for a week, Lesal carefully snuck to the lobby to grab a copy of the New York Times. Rushing back to his room, the thug read about the shooting spree back home and turned pale. It was perfectly clear as to what was going on in Manhattan. As he had expected, his criminal cohorts were scouring the region looking to collect the sizeable reward on his head.

Throwing the paper on the floor in disgust, Lesal muttered, *"Jeezus, I'd better get my ass in gear and finish my job before they waste me."*

CHAPTER 27
AXEL GILAN

Axel Gilan sat on his bed, assembling all the paraphernalia he would need for his venture. Passport, stacks of money, a variety of guns and knives, and his favorite pair of brass knuckles for good luck were neatly packed into his suitcase. The one item he lacked was a clue to Lesal's whereabouts.

As he sat stewing over his dilemma, Mr. Gilan became increasingly annoyed. Axel had worked extremely hard his entire life become the boss of his syndicate. It was exasperating for him to be demoted to a mere hitman again. To the irritated mob boss, being relegated to menial criminal labor was both vulgar and demeaning. Brooding over his distasteful obligation, he reflected back to his early life and introduction to the syndicate.

Hours after Axel was born, the infant was left on the doorstep of a local mobster in Staten Island in lieu of a payment on a debt. The child was raised in an atmosphere of brazen crime and corruption which became completely customary to the young boy. By the time he could walk, he accompanied his doting father on most of his business affairs and witnessed his first hit at the age of five.

To the young and gullible Axel, criminal life seemed fun and exciting, and he begged his dad for a weapon of his own. With his never-ending whining becoming a continual irritation to his father, he was finally given a single shot derringer with strict instructions not to use it unless absolutely necessary.

Not long after being given his first firearm, the boy and his father were ambushed in a back alley by a rival goon. Axel watched carefully as his father stood immobile with a 9mm pointed at his head.

As the arrogant hooligan mocked and insulted his father mercilessly, Axel slowly pulled the tiny pistol out of his pocket. With the bullying thug's attention directed solely at his father, the child fired the tiny firearm, hitting the man squarely in the groin.

Writhing on the asphalt in agony, the wounded mobster cursed at the impressionable young child, *"You filthy little rat bastard. You shot my nads clear into Jersey."*

Retrieving the downed mobster's weapon from the blacktop, his father handed it to Axel saying, *"Good job my faithful son. Now it's time for you to finish what you started."*

With his hand shaking unsteadily, the boy could barely hold up the full-sized gun. Taking a wobbly aim at the stupefied gangster, he fired his first shot, blowing the man's right ear completely off. The second blast took off three fingers of the goons left hand.

Momentarily frustrated by his miss-aims, little Axel grasped the firearm with both hands. He slowly walked up to his screaming victim and fired point blank. The bullet carved a four-inch diameter hole through the man's chest.

Entirely impressed by his young child's courage and resolve, the boy's father knelt before his son and solemnly pronounced, *"As of today, you are a man, and I could not be any prouder of you. From this day forward, you shall be known as "the Axe."*

The poignant childhood memories made Axel grin for a moment.

His first kill seemed like a hundred years ago, and he had off'd countless adversaries since. While dragging his luggage to the car, he got an idea. Thinking that there might be a clue as to Lesal's whereabouts at his apartment, Axel headed to Brooklyn.

After breaking down the door of the squalid apartment, his eyes slowly surveyed the dingy room. With the place in shambles, it looked like Mr. Spurnell had left in a big hurry. He slowly picked his way through the clutter to the bedroom door. When he opened it and turned on the light, he gasped.

The walls were covered in red painted writing and the repeated threats were clearly those of a completely deranged individual. "Kill Zane Worth," and "Zane Worth must die," were brushed maniacally over all the walls and ceiling. In a corner, was a shrine of sorts with pictures and newspaper articles of a conductor named Franco Maximilian. The photos were attached to the wall with ice picks and switchblades, the weapons piercing the unknown man's skull. Knowing his gruesome goon all too well, it was obvious that Lesal had been stalking this unknown mark with the intention of murdering him.

Axel took out his mobile phone and typed in the name Zane Worth in the search bar. His rap sheet and several photos appeared with information about his sentencing for attempted robbery of a bank in Oklahoma. Looking further down the page, it appeared that he had escaped during a prison breakout and had been on the lamb ever since.

Axel compared Zane's mug shot to the pictures of Franco Maximilian on the wall. Other than Zane's shaved head in the prison photo, the faces were very similar. The only odd discrepancy was that the Spanish conductor seemed to have only one arm, and Zane Worth obviously had two.

Scratching his head, he pondered over the perplexing anomaly for a few moments. After comparing the two faces one last time, he was convinced that Zane Worth and Franco Maximilian were the same man, no matter how many arms he had.

He also realized if he could find this escaped felon, turned orchestra conductor; Lesal would not be far behind.

Turning on Mr. Spurnell's computer, Axel started typing an email, entering a series of contacts from a piece of paper taken from his wallet.

On the tattered list were the addresses of every syndicate boss from Boston to Shanghai. With a new agenda in mind, he posted a personal reward of one million dollars for any information on the whereabouts of Lesal Spurnell and Franco Maximilian.

He made it perfectly clear that the men were to be located, and most importantly, left alive. If either were killed, no remuneration would be paid. He wanted to avoid another blood bath, since too much attention had already been directed toward his crime organization. He then attached both the mug shots of Zane, as well as a scanned picture from time magazine cover. After including a recent photo of Lesal Spurnell, he hit the send button.

As he sat in the gloom of the blubbery goon's apartment planning his next move, Axel smiled. Getting back on the computer, he booked a one-way ticket to Arizona.

The New York winters had always depressed him, so he had decided to head for a warmer climate while he waited for information to filter in. A small southwestern town like Tucson seemed like the perfect place to hang out incognito. He booked a suite in an exclusive resort near Sabino Canyon and signed off.

"Time to get out of this rat trap, and snare my pesky, plump problem," he thought amusedly. *"My dear Lesal, it's about time you retired permanently."*

CHAPTER 28
LESAL'S BIG BREAK

As Lesal Spurnell lounged on his bed, searching the internet for any clue to Zane's hiding place, he started to feel like he was quickly losing his sanity.

After being locked inside his room for weeks, he was getting a severe case of cabin fever. He knew if he stayed couped up inside for another minute, he would gladly blow his brains out and save his boss some cash. Reaching into the closet, he grabbed his oversized suitcase of disguises.

After picking out a formfitting, purple satin dress, the mobster grabbed a cheesy, red wig and started dressing. After slathering on a pound of makeup, and slapping on a healthy dose of Channel #5, he strutted his way to the cab line in front of the hotel.

After stuffing his shimmering, oversized backside into the taxi, Lesal barked, *"Take me to the trendiest bar in town, and make it quick!"* Without a moment's hesitation, the cabbie replied, *"Si Senora, I know a very good place, and I will get you there on the double! Bye the way, I must say you look simply ravishing tonight."*

Not quite sure if he was being mocked or hit on, Lesal snarled back, *"Just keep your eyes on the road you miserable, flea-bitten mongrel."*

A half hour later, the cab arrived at a swanky, neon-wrapped night club called *Mafioso's*. Spurnell chucked under his breath upon seeing the sign, then hopped out anxiously from the car. Tossing the cabbie a fifty, he pranced his way past the door bouncer who was far too stunned at the disquieting sight to ask for Lesal's identification.

Swishing up to the bar, Lesal ordered a Sloe gin on the rocks. Turning around to survey the club, a frown forming on his face. *"What a dump!"* spewed from his lips, as he tried to sip daintily on his drink.

"What the hell, I'm just here to mingle and get drunk, so who gives a crap what the joint looks like," he harped to himself.

A few minutes later, an inebriated local man cautiously approached the sparkling monstrosity. He offered to buy the rotund, purple clad assassin a cocktail, saying reverently, *"You are the most beautiful woman I have ever seen. Where have you been hiding all my life?"*

Lesal instantly smirked.

No longer trying to disguise his voice, he growled, *"Oh, I've been around."*

"I'm surprised you've never seen me because I'm usually at your mother's house, humping her brains out. So why don't you just shut your ugly mug and get lost!" For a split-second, his admirer was speechless. After realizing that his saintly mother's honor had been inexcusably violated, he stepped back in anger.

Cocking his fist, the irate man attempted to punch the insulting American whore for her disparaging remark. To be certain, Lesal Spurnell was not a man to be trifled with. With lightning swiftness, he turned to his attacker, quickly kneeing him squarely in the groin.

As the man fell to the floor in agony, Lesal laughed heartily, pulling his dress back down over his bountiful buttocks. Turning to the bartender, he cooed, *"My, My! You Mexico City men don't seem to have any manners what-so-ever!"*

In the far corner of the establishment, a stylishly dressed Mexican man had been watching Lesal and the bar fight intently. He ordered his associate to approach the mysterious woman and invite him to his table.

When his subordinate reached Lesal, he relayed his bosses request. The thug shook his head affirmatively, then responded stridently, *"That's fine by me. Just remember to keep those drinks coming!"*

After Lesal had sashayed to his table, the mysterious man introduced himself.

"My name is Don Rafael Christio. I have been observing you all evening, and I must say you handled yourself very well with that rude drunk. You are quite agile and fierce for being such a good-looking, full figured woman."

Spurnell frowned, replying in falsetto, *"My glass seems to be empty."*

Clicking his fingers to get the bar tender's attention, the Don continued.

"Perhaps you would like to accompany me to my hacienda for a night cap? There, we could get to know each other much better."

Lesal giggled coyly. *"Oh no, I am not that kind of girl, my dear Don."* Smiling back, the well-mannered man questioned slyly, *"So, exactly what kind of girl are you?"*

Lesal gave his admirer a steely glare, replying, *"A very thirsty one."*

The two characters continued to drink and banter back and forth for hours until Lesal Spurnell was completely smashed.

During the good-humored repartee, he had foolishly conveyed the story of his quest to hunt down Zane Worth, aka: Franco Maximilian. The Don listened intently but seemed to be inwardly amused. Once he felt the floor starting to tilt and spin, Lesal decided he needed to get back to the safety of his hotel suite before he passed out cold.

Getting up unsteadily from the table, the soused thug thanked his generous host for a wonderful evening, gushing, *"My dear Don, you are both a chivalrous and most entertaining gentleman. Unfortunately, I must return to my hotel and get my beauty sleep."* Don Christo frowned at the news, then gave a curious reply.

"My dear lady, I know of an American who owns a beach taberna in Puerto Vallarta. He had dark curly hair, blue eyes, and was missing an arm. I met him there not four months ago while visiting some associates of mine. If I were you, I would checkout the lead. Perhaps this is the man you seek."

The news of Zane's location sobered up Lesal like a fall through lake ice in January.

He blew the Don a clumsy kiss and stumbled to the front door as fast as his stumpy legs could move in high heels. Before he exited the night club, he turned, braying loudly, *"My sweetest Don, I don't know how I can ever repay you for your kindness!"*

Don Christo smiled back, responding with a heartfelt *"Via con Dios me Amiga."*

Once Lesal had left the building, Don Rafael Christo mumbled cagily, *"Don't you worry, my plump prize, for I do know of a way that you can repay me. I promise, we shall meet again very soon, my stunning vision of perfection."*

CHAPTER 29
DON RAFAEL CHRISTO

DON RAFAEL CHRISTO WAS an extremely powerful man with many diverse interests and talents.

First and foremost, he was the kingpin of the Mexico City Mafia. He ruled over his highly lucrative domain with an iron fist and had had personally murdered hundreds of his rivals without blinking an eye. Over the years, he had amassed a fortune in the billions by controlling both the Mexican crime syndicate, and every important government official in the country. The man was so completely untouchable that even the FBI, CIA, and Interpol gave him a very wide berth.

The crime lord was also an avid collector of rare and unique things, and whatever Don Christo desired, he obtained. From palatial estates to the finest collectable cars, the Don either purchased his prizes, or simply took them without reservation.

He also enjoyed controlling the lives of people he found entertaining, either by coercion, or extortion.

The Don viewed people much like puppets, inanimate play things that he could easily manipulate. Unfortunately for his toys, when he was no longer amused at pulling the strings of his human marionettes, he would simply dispose of them, never to be seen again.

A more secretive side to the Don was in his apparent fondness for drag queens. The man seemed utterly fascinated with the concept of grown men dressing up as tasteless and gaudy females. Even more bizarre, the fatter and uglier the feux women were, the more captivated he became.

This abnormal enchantment began soon after his much-adored mother had passed away. After her untimely death, the Don scoured each and every drag bar in Mexico looking for a performer who resembled his blessed Mamacita.

Once he had located a short, brutish, and overweight female impersonator bearing a close resemblance to his mother, he would simply kidnap them and take them back to his palatial estate.

The bewildered and helpless men were then forced to play the role of his saintly creator. If the petrified performers botched up their motherly duties, Don Christo would first drape the ill-fated failures in irons. After giving them a ride aboard his helicopter, he would push them unceremoniously into the Pacific Ocean.

Don Christo's heart-wrenching search for the perfect mother replacement was both unrelenting and highly disturbing.

On that fateful night when Lesal had accidentally stumbled into his bar, Don Christo had been instantly enraptured. The boorish, scar-faced, and overstuffed woman appeared to be a carbon copy of his sacred Madre.

After spending several hours with Lesal, the Don had been completely smitten. Lesal's gravelly voice and unrefined mannerisms had been a perfect match. Minutes after meeting the brutish assassin, the Mexican mobster had already started scheming of how to ensnare his future parental stand-in.

When the highly intoxicated hitman had inadvertently spilled the beans about his hunt for Zane, the Don was simply beside himself with delight. He had quickly recalled the email that Axel Gilan had posted on line looking for information on Lesal Spurnell and Zane Worth. It hadn't taken the crafty Latin crime lord long to put two and two together.

Don Christo signaled to his man servant, gesturing his need for a phone. He then took out a small address book and dialed a number. Fifteen minutes later, he hung up the phone with a diabolical grin.

Rapping his glass with a spoon, Don Rafael Christo happily announced, *"Free drinks for everyone, for this has been a most momentous day!"*

"Let us toast to my resurrected saintly mother, Mama Lesalitta."

CHAPTER 30
HAVOC IN PUERTO VALLARTA

EARLY THE NEXT MORNING, Lesal packed his suitcase and rushed out of the hotel. The rotund assassin was still wearing his bedazzled sausage of a dress and mussed up wig from the previous evening. With so many paid assassins on the hunt for him, he thought it best to stay in disguise while out in the open.

He arrived in Puerto Vallarta three hours later; quickly renting a small room in a seedy motel in the heart of old town.

That evening, he wandered into a local bar and started asking the clientele questions about the whereabouts of Zane Worth. Within minutes, Lesal had learned the location of his marks beach cantina.

Lesal left the taberna at midnight and returned to his room. Highly energized by the news he had gleaned, he stayed up until the wee hours of the morning plotting the final details of his long-sought revenge.

After receiving a fortuitous phone call from Don Christo, Axel Gilan realized that he would now be able to rid himself of Lesal once and for all. He was even more pleased upon hearing the terms of the proposal. In lieu of collecting the sizeable cash reward, the Don had agreed to resolve Axel's dilemma for him free of charge.

Hurriedly packing his travel bags, Axel was flying to Mexico to make sure that Don Raphael Christo would live up to his promise. Since mobsters had a reputation for being less than honorable from time to time, the syndicate boss was going to monitor the situation personally.

Once Lesal Spurnell was out of the picture, he had also devised an underhanded plan to claim a valuable prize of his own.

Zane's renewed life in Mexico was one of leisure and contentment.

With Lumpy and Slim running the show, all Zane had to do was mingle, drink, and flirt shamelessly with the guests.

Knowing that Lesal Spurnell was locked up tight in prison for the rest of his life, Zane finally had time to relax and enjoy his well-deserved retirement.

Not in a million years, would it have crossed his mind that he was still being hunted by his dreaded nemesis.

Axel Gilan and Don Christo arrived in Puerto Vallarta a few hours after Lesal Spurnell.

They met briefly to solidify the deal, and quickly sent out their minions to locate the two targets.

Since Axel was well aware of Mr. Spurnell's dubious talent for disguising himself in female camouflage, the thug was located quickly. Zane was spotted hitting on a cute blonde tourist at his cantina.

With both men on the radar screen, the orders were to keep them both under constant surveillance. If Lesal was spotted getting into a water taxi and heading south toward Zane's establishment, the plan was to be initiated.

Lesal awoke the next morning with a crooked grin plastered over his disfigured face.

He had been waiting a very long time to enact his reprisal and he could barely contain his enthusiasm. After a hearty breakfast of huevos rancheros and chorizo, he returned to his room to dress.

Digging through his stash of disguises, he pulled out a neon yellow, one-piece ladies swim suit made of Lycra spandex. After squeezing into the blindingly bright swimwear, he started packing the inside of the suit with cotton padding, increasing the size of his breasts and backside three-fold.

Looking much like a giant mutant lemon, he started covering his exposed skin with dark skin bronzer. After smearing on a jar of rouge, and applying flaming coral colored lipstick, he clipped on a pair of large gold-hoop earrings.

To top off the flamboyant disguise, he placed a large floppy hat on his head and donned a pair of highly ornate, oversized sunglasses.

When he checked out his hideous beach babe makeover in the mirror, he laughed heartily.

He now looked exactly like all the other overfed, sunbaked, rich female visitors splayed over the beach like a rookery of elephant seals.

After grabbing a matching yellow beach bag, he then carefully packed his revolver in a towel. Once finished with his preparations, Lesal waddled out of his room and headed toward the docks.

Flashing a wad of cash, he ordered the boat captain to take him to Zane's beachside bar.

As he stumbled awkwardly into the water taxi, the clumsy cutthroat almost tipped the entire craft over. The quick-thinking boat pilot grabbed Lesal's arm and helped him to his seat.

Immediately pissed off, the contemptuous crank sputtered angrily, *"Keep your filthy hands off me you smelly ape."* The captain shrugged meekly, responding, *"Sorry, Senora. I was only trying to save my boat."*

Spurnell huffed with disdain and pointed south, shouting, *"Move it, you half-witted monkey!"* The Captain scowled, muttering back under his breath, *"Si, estupido vaca gorda."*

Arriving at the bar's dock, Lesal climbed awkwardly out of the boat. When the Captain asked for his fare, Lesal tossed a twenty into a dirty puddle of water on the floor of the boat. As the assassin sauntered provocatively toward the bar, the irked captain flipped him off with both hands, then pocketed the soggy cash with a scowl.

The stunned crowd could not help but stare at the screaming yellow nightmare as she approached the cantina. Always the consummate host, Zane welcomed her warmly and asked what she would like to drink.

Singing in falsetto, Lesal asked what the specialty of the house was. Zane barked at Lumpy to make a *"Colada Extravaganza."* Once the foo-foo drink was served, Zane asked the customers to toast to the new guest's continued good health. With a hearty cheer by all, Zane returned to his other guests.

Lesal sat at the bar, trying desperately to stay in character. He had an uncontrollable urge to grab his gun and plug Zane with all six bullets but knew this was not the time or place.

By the end of the afternoon, the guzzling goon had downed six or seven *Extravaganza's* and was starting to feel the drinks dizzying effects.

Emboldened by the excess alcohol to finish his quest, Lesal waved at Zane to get his attention. *"My dear Mister Worth, could you help me get back to my hotel? I would attempt the trip myself, but that last nasty taxi captain made a pass at me and I'm terrified it might happen again."*

Zane graciously agreed, knowing that the roundtrip took around twenty minutes. He was sure there would be plenty of time to return before the sunset crowd started to arrive.

Carefully taking hold Lesal's pudgy arm, Zane announced, *"We will take my personal craft, so you won't have to deal with any of the lecherous locals."*

Once the boat was well out in the bay, Lesal quietly reached into his bag and grabbed his gun. Zane had been watching the horizon for oncoming boats and didn't see the underhanded fat femme fatale draw a weapon until it was too late.

Zane's jaw dropped when the beastly tourist took off her hat and sun glasses.

"So, we finally meet again, Mr. Worth. I have been waiting a very long time for this moment. You have no idea what you've put me through during my mission to find you, but you are going to pay the ultimate price for your evasion. You have ruined my life and profession, and for that, I am going to kill you where you sit."

"Please don't feel too sorry for yourself. Because of you, I now have a price on my head and will probably be off'd by my own mob at any time."

"To tell you truth; I no longer care if I die. My only satisfaction is

in knowing your sorry ass didn't get the best of me. I will happily perish knowing that I was still the best assassin in the history of the syndicate."

Petrified with fear, Zane sat motionless as he thought frantically of a way out. With his eyes locked on his nemesis, Lesal raised the weapon and pointed it at his victim's forehead.

"You should have come with me when you had the chance. We are much alike, and I think we would have made an invincible team. Since you refused to cooperate, all I can say now is good bye and good riddance."

Zane covered his face when he heard the gun fire.

A few seconds later, when he realized he was still breathing, he peeked through his fingers hesitantly. With his heart stuck in his throat, he saw Lesal Spurnell grinning crazily like a chimpanzee on crack.

"Sorry, but I just changed my mind. After thinking the situation over, I believe you haven't suffered half as much as I have. No, it's time you experienced some real pain of your own."

With a maniacal look of amusement, he continued.

"First, I am going to shoot your remaining arm. As you're screaming in pain, and pleading for mercy, I'm going to shoot your right leg, then the left."

"When I've had a small taste of sweet retribution, I will throw your bleeding body off this boat and watch you flail around, trying desperately to remain afloat. As you tire, and the excruciating pain in your extremities overtakes your will to live, I will watch as you slowly sink below the waves with a contented grin. If I'm really lucky, a passing shark might help pull you under."

"Now let the games begin."

Lesal slowly pointed his gun at his victim's arm. A second later, Zane heard the sharp discharge of the weapon and cringed. After waiting a second, he was amazed to feel nothing.

On the other hand, the mobster started screaming bloody murder, and shook his hand like it was on fire. As Lesal continued to curse a blue streak, and unexpected sound was heard.

Over the distinctive hum of approaching outboard motors, a loud speaker blared out, *"Lesal Spurnell, put your hands in the air."* Zane turned around to see a pair of Mexican police cruisers closing in rapidly in their direction. After seeing the speeding boats near, Zane assumed that a sharpshooter on one of the crafts had blasted the gun from the grumpy goons' fingers.

When Lesal realized his plans were being foiled, he lunged for Zane, grabbing him by the throat.

"So help me God, I will crush the life out of you before anyone can save you."

No longer in fear of being shot, Zane had endured more than enough of Lesal Spurnell's crap.

He drew back his head, butting Lesal in the forehead with all his strength. The fat man's eyes drew back in his head, and he quickly let go of his mark. By the time the hefty hood had come to, the police boats had pulled aside. Two of the Mexican officers jumped into Zane's craft and quickly handcuffed Lesal.

As Zane watched in utter confusion, two well-dressed men stepped into his boat.

Lesal's eyes almost popped out when he recognized his mob boss, Axel Gilan. When he saw Don Christo as well, he was completely dumbfounded. When the porky assassin finally figured out he had been two-timed, he glared at the Don with utter contempt.

With his temper boiling over, he screamed, *"You filthy bastard, you set me up."* Don Christo smiled back coyly, responding, *"Perhaps. But in doing so, I have saved your life."*

As Lesal struggled, still sputtering and swearing, Don Raphael Christo calmly pulled out a Taser from his jacket pocket and shoved it on Lesal's forehead.

As the angry sparks in Lesal's bloated eyes quickly dimmed, the Don leaned over and whispered lovingly into his ear, *"Sweet dreams my precious trophy."* The two attending officers grabbed the paralyzed hood by his arms and dragged him into one of the police boats.

With Lesal secured and out of the way, the American mob boss turned to address Zane.

"My name is Axel Gilan, and I am Lesal's supervisor. Whether you realize it or not, you have caused me a shitload of trouble."

Before Zane could ask what was going on, *the Axe* pulled out a syringe from his shirt pocket, skillfully planting it in Zane's neck.

CHAPTER 31
LESAL SPURNELL'S SWAN SONG

SWEATING PROFUSELY, LESAL SPURNELL awoke from a vivid nightmare.

In his dream, he had been hanging from a rope suspended over a deep crevasse. As he clung on in desperation, Zane Worth was shaking and tugging at the cable from above, trying to knock him off. A thousand feet below, a tangled bed of jagged glass chards and razor-sharp knife blades were pointing skyward to catch the gangster's impending fall.

As the rope slowly started slipping from Lesal's grasp, his adversary looked down at him, taunting, *"No matter how hard you try, you will never catch me. I'm smarter than you and more of a criminal than you'll ever be. Lesal Spurnell, it's time for you admit that you have failed in your task! I will watch you die, then live out the rest of my life like a king!"*

When his hands finally lost their grip, Lesal looked up, screaming, *"You haven't won yet. One way or another, I will kill you, Zane Worth!"*

As he plummeted toward to his grisly demise, the defeated mobster was horrified to realize that he had failed, and his archenemy had inexplicably gotten the best of him.

Still shaken from the portentous dream, Lesal slowly rubbed his eyes and started focusing about the gloomy room.

The unfamiliar walls were covered in hodgepodge of family photographs and ornate crucifixes. Over the fireplace was an oil painting of an old woman who looked oddly familiar. When Lesal gazed down, he was floored to see he was wearing a simple black frock with a white, laced collar. A pair of woman's black flats were stuffed on his feet.

Shaking the cobwebs from his head, he swung his legs to the floor. Unexpectedly, the sound of rattling chains was heard. The sight of metal shackles secured to his ankles sent his mind reeling.

Feeling entirely perplexed, the gangster stumbled to the dresser and looked into the mirror. Perched atop his head was a simple black wig with a braided bun on top.

The sight made his volatile temper erupt. Lesal grabbed at the hair with both hands and struggled violently to yank it off. To his amazement, it seemed to be permanently glued to his head.

Having an eerie feeling, he looked into the mirror again. Without a doubt, he looked like someone's burly and dowdy grandmother. Slowly turning his head, he looked back at the portrait on the wall and froze.

The matronly face in the painting looked exactly like his. Completely baffled, he shouted anxiously, *"What in hell is going on here?"*

As he stood at the mirror, shifting his glance furtively from the picture to his repugnant reflection, the door to his bedroom opened and Don Christo entered.

"Good morning my Dear Lesal. I hope you slept well. As you can already see, I took the liberty of having you dressed in some new attire. I hope you find it becoming."

All the mobster could do is gasp out, *"I don't understand any of this."* The Don smiled mischievously and started to enlighten him on his situation.

"My precious Lesal, the night that you walked into my nightclub, I knew I had finally found the surrogate that I had been dreaming about.

"Since my mother's tragic death, I have been on the hunt for the ideal substitution for my precious Mamacita. Over the past two years, I have scoured every drag bar in Mexico, yet never finding the exact woman to take her place. When I heard your gravelly voice, and saw your disfigured face, it was like standing before my blessed mother, raised from her grave."

"Are you nuts?" Lesal sputtered contemptuously. *"I'm not your ugly dead mother, and I never will be."*

Luckily, Don Christo ignored Mr. Spurnell's unwise slur and continued.

"Unfortunately, you have no choice in the matter. I made a deal with your boss, Axel Gilan. In lieu of collecting the substantial reward upon your death, I traded your boss's cash for the possession of your life. You will do whatever I request or suffer the consequences."

To prove his veiled threat, the Don pushed the button on the light panel.

A screen descended from a slot in the ceiling and from the opposite wall, the beam of a projector came to life. As Lesal watched in horror, men dressed in similar attire to his own, and bound tightly in chains, were screaming in terror as the Don pushed them from a helicopter to their watery graves.

After seeing the seventh victim plunging to certain death, Lesal could no longer watch the gruesome video.

"They were all my past disappointments, and I disposed of them

where they will never be found. For your own sake, I hope you pass my test. I would hate to be forced to murder my ideal motherly replacement."

Lesal stood silently for a few moments. With the reality of the Don's video choking his mind with dread, he peeped, *"What do you want me to do?"*

"As my doting and devoted mother, you will wash and iron my clothes. When I am dirty, you shall help bathe me. When I am hungry, you will cook and clean up for me. If you are wise, my stomach should never growl, and my house will sparkle and shine at all times."

"If I happen to fail at a task, you will encourage and nurture me like any devoted parent. When I am sad, you will hold me. When I am happy, you will laugh with me. In each and every way, you will be my angelic mother."

"If you fail at your mission, so be it. I will gladly shove you from my helicopter and watch the sharks feed on your overabundant flesh."

As Lesal absorbed the reality of his new duties, he shuddered. He was now convinced that the Don was a stark raving madman. He was also certain that there was no way he could escape his fate. If he tried to run, he was convinced he would be quickly recaptured by the ruthless mob boss and his crew of cutthroats.

As the bleakness of his future penetrated his brain, Lesal finally acquiesced. He knew he was trapped inside an inescapable nightmare and helplessly subject to the whims and wishes of a certifiable lunatic. He was certain that nothing short of death could save him now.

Looking up gloomily, Lesal slowly muttered with a raspy sigh, *"My sweet Son, what would you like for dinner?"* His demented captor smiled broadly, replying, *"Your superb pollo con arroz would be wonderful, Mama."*

With a spine-chilling look of madness flooding his soulless eyes, Don Raphael Christo tenderly grasped Lesal by the arm and whispered reverently, *"Blessed Mother, I'm so very happy that you have finally returned to me, and I vow to God never to lose you again. No matter what evils life may throw at us, I swear upon my grave that we shall remain together forever!"*

For the first time in his adult life, a single tear of remorse started to roll down Lesal's sagging cheek. With his leg chains rattling in mocking cruelty, the once arrogant and coldblooded assassin hobbled slowly toward the door in search of the kitchen.

As he shuffled passed Don Christo, he softly cursed under his breath, *"I should have blown my brains out back in Vegas when I had the chance."*

CHAPTER 32
TOPSY-TURVY

THE SOUND OF BILLOWING curtains rustling softly in the balmy afternoon breeze slowly awoke Zane Worth.

As he looked about his surroundings, he found himself lying in an unfamiliar room, then quickly catching the pungent smell of sea air. Craning his neck to look out the window, he could see small fishing boats in the distance, bobbing peacefully in turquoise-green waters.

Dazed and disoriented, he tried to get out of bed but quickly fell back, the stabbing pain in his chest holding him hostage. As a wave of panic washed over him, he shouted out, *"Is anyone there? I need help."* A few seconds later, the door opened, and a petite Mexican woman dressed in nurses attire entered his room and started nagging.

"Silencio, Signor. Ju muss be berry quiet, for ju are bery sic and need jur rest. We don't want ju to hab anober art attack!"

With a stern look, the nurse handed him a small paper cup with some medication. *"Take deez now and ju will feel mas better!"*

He downed the pills and tried to get some answers from his pesky caretaker. The nurse quickly put a finger to her lips, motioning for him to go to sleep. A few minutes later he started feeling warm and fuzzy.

With his brain careening with questions, his eyes slowly shut, and he drifted off into the murky twilight.

When Zane's eyes reopened, it was now evening. The room was dimly illuminated by single table lamp in the far corner. When the hair on his arm started to rise, his sixth sense warned him that something was awry. Turning his head back, he gasped when he saw a man standing silently behind him.

"Hey, take it easy Zane. For your own sake, try to keep calm. My name is Axel Gilan, and we met a few days ago on your boat."

Zane slowly began to remember who the man was. An instant later, he panicked again. Thinking that Lesal Spurnell might be somewhere close, he tried to get up, but the pain was excruciating.

Axel chuckled softly. *"Please relax. You don't want to pull out your stitches."*

With the ache in his chest throbbing mercilessly, Zane gingerly pulled the front of his gown down. To his amazement, there were two lengthy incisions, the sutures still raw and oozing with droplets of blood. *"What in hell happened to me?"* he moaned feebly.

Axel pulled up a chair and sat down next to Zane. *"I think this is a good time to fill you in on everything you need to know."*

"As you may remember, Lesal Spurnell once worked for me and my organization." *"Unfortunately, because of his particular line of work, the Feds were trying to capture and pump him for information about my syndicate. Being such a liability, I could no longer afford to keep Lesal around. When he escaped from his safe house, I placed a sizeable hit on him in an attempt to silence the man for good."*

"I had no idea that my plan would backfire so badly"

"Many innocent people died; their only crime was in looking

somewhat similar to my pudgy protégé. After the initial killing spree, the cops went crazy. We had to shut down our entire operation and go into hiding."

"I called off the hit on Mr. Spurnell and offered a reward for information on his whereabouts. After breaking into his apartment, I found a shine of sorts, devoted to your demise. It seemed clear that Lesal was hell-bent on killing you, but I was not clear as to why."

"I offered a reward for information on you as well, knowing that wherever you were hiding, my assassin was sure to be close behind."

"A fellow business associate soon located Lesal in Mexico and contacted me. In lieu of the reward, Don Cristo insisted on taking personal possession of Lesal. He promised me that Mr. Spurnell would be kept under lock and key where the law could never touch him."

"Knowing the Don's reputation for getting what he wanted, one way or another, I dared not refuse his request. We met in Puerto Vallarta and kept tabs on you and Lesal. We knew when he boarded a boat and headed to your bar dressed in disguise, he was on a mission to waste you."

"The Don made a quick call to the Mexican police and they provided us with two boats and unquestioned assistance. The rest of the story you know."

Zane turned deathly pale as he listened to the Axel's tale of intrigue.

He hadn't realized that Lesal had escaped and was still on his trail. He shuddered when he recalled how close he had come to being murdered. He had mistakenly assumed that he was safe and secure from the diabolical monster's clutches.

After hearing that Lesal Spurnell had been taken out of the picture permanently, he breathed a huge sigh of relief.

Upon Axel's insistence, Zane told his fraught ridden story from the day he and Lesal had first met. Axel listened in silent amazement to his trials and tribulations in trying to evade Lesal.

With a stunned look, the mob boss commented, *"To my knowledge, you are the only man to have ever escaped from Lesal Spurnell. I must admit that is quite a unique accomplishment. Perhaps I have made a wise choice."*

"Since Lesal Spurnell will no longer a problem for either of us, I believe you now owe me a favor."

"You must realize that I have lost a valuable subordinate, and you owe me your life for saving you from Lesal's clutches. I am not sure what you did to aggravate him to such an extent, but you are incredibly lucky that I intervened before he killed you."

Zane touched his chest gingerly, and then looked up at Axel.

"What happened to me on the boat?" Turning deadly serious, Axel enlightened Zane on his new career path.

"To repay your debt to me, you are now under my employ. It seemed clear to me that any man who could thwart Lesal at his own game would make a great assassin. I will train you on all you need to know about the business, and you will perform whatever task I request."

Zane's mind started swimming, and he couldn't believe his ears.

"Mr. Gilan, what if I refuse? It's not that I'm extremely grateful for your help, but I really have no desire to work for the mob. In all honesty, I just want to be left alone to live out the rest of my life in peace."

Axel took out a small remote-control devise from his pocket and casually pushed a red button.

Instantly, Zane started feeling weak and lightheaded. After breaking out in an ice-cold sweat, he felt as though his life was slowly seeping from his body. As the light in the room started to grow dim, he looked up at Axel in a panic. The man smiled at him coldly and pushed the button once more. Within seconds, Zane started to feel much better.

"I'm sorry to make my point in such a cruel manner, but you had to understand the consequences of your refusal."

"After I injected you with a powerful tranquilizer, my men brought you here to a small private hospital outside of Cancun. I flew in a doctor who owed me a favor, and he performed some minor surgery at my behest."

"You now have two devices implanted in your chest. One is a powerful GPS transmitter. The other is a simple pacemaker with an additional feature. If I push this button, the pacemaker starts to slow. If I push the other button, it stops functioning altogether. The devises are interconnected, so wherever you are, I have the ability to locate you and terminate your life without notice."

"Please don't feel like I am being distrustful. After dealing with Lesal's instabilities, and the potentially disastrous consequences if he had spilled his guts to the authorities, I have had all my employees implanted with the same type of devise. Upon my request, all the other syndicate bosses have agreed to act accordingly."

"Now, I no longer have to worry about anyone in the organization betraying me or the other consortiums. I have to say I find this new technology simply ingenious."

"I must warn you that the devise should not be tampered with. If anyone beside my doctor tries to remove your pacemaker, it will short-circuit, and you will expire immediately."

"You will be required to have minor surgery every few years to replace the power cells. Let's hope your special heart doctor remains healthy for an exceedingly long time."

Zane was left speechless, trying desperately to absorb the unbelievable information.

His all-too-familiar feeling of depression descended over him like a soul chilling fog. After all the trials he had gone through; to end up becoming an assassin for the mob was simply ludicrous.

Until now, he had beaten the odds and survived all the obstacles to his happiness. Inexplicably, in a heartbeat, his carefree life had been stolen away because of Lesal Spurnell and his despicable antics.

At that moment of clarity, a diabolical urge hidden deep within his soul slowly started coming to life.

Realizing there was no way out of the desperate situation; he turned his head boldly to face to his new boss and agreed to his terms of employment.

Axel grinned, replying, *"A very wise choice my friend!"*

CHAPTER 33
THE RESURRECTION OF
MAESTRO MAXIMILIAN

When Zane Worth's surgical wounds had healed, he returned to New York City with Axel Gilan.

After months of intensive training, Zane had mastered all Axel's lessons on becoming a professional mob assassin. His mentor had been most impressed with his student's accomplishments and felt confident that Zane would perform his various deadly duties with great expertise.

As the ideal cover, Zane returned to being Maestro Franco Maximilian. Axel used his extensive worldwide influence to book Franco in countries where his underworld services were needed.

After finishing a sold-out concert of *Mahler's* fifth symphony in Zurich, Zane combed the twisting, back alleys of the ancient Swiss city on the hunt for his mark. His kills were always quick and clean, and he was ever mindful to leave no trace of his misdeeds.

Unlike Lesal Spurnell, Zane did not enjoy first terrorizing, then offing his victims. To him, being a professional assassin was a tasteless and degrading occupation. The faster he could complete his sordid task, the better he felt about himself.

With his third phenomenally successful concert, and well executed mob hit completed, Axel allowed Zane to return to his home in Puerto Vallarta for some rest and relaxation.

Zane sat quietly in his first-class seat, staring blankly at his meal. Not in the mood to eat, he started to reflect over his new career. He had concluded that when your life was at stake, you would do anything in your power to stay alive. After all, that was only human nature. To kill or be killed really left you no viable choice in the matter.

On the brighter side, his conducting engagements gave him a slightly more desirable purpose and the opportunity to live a lifestyle that most people could only dream of.

What bothered him the most was that his very existence was now held in the capricious hands of his boss, Axel Gilan. He knew perfectly well that any slipup on his mob duties would set his fate.

Zane never doubted that his new life held no guarantees of peace and happiness, but he hadn't had a good night's sleep since his new profession had begun.

That familiar feeling of all-encompassing dread hovered steadfastly over his head. He felt as though Lesal Spurnell's ghost was still nipping at his heels. He was constantly nauseous and on edge. His gut churned with angst and fiery acid chewed relentlessly at his throat.

He glanced down to his plate and absently started playing with his mashed potatoes. Before he could stop himself, he had traced an unhappy face in the insipid mound of spuds. With uncontained rage welling up from within, he pounded the despicable reminder of Lesal Spurnell with his fist.

The sound of shattering of china alerted the flight attendant who came running up.

"Sir, is everything alright?" she purred, as she started wiping the mess off the floor. Zane looked at her with a glazed look, responding, *"Sorry, it was a stupid accident. I don't know what came over me."*

When the attendant departed, Zane mumbled irritably," *I just realized that I have left one very urgent task unfinished."*

The three ex-convicts were sharing a bucket of iced beers along with several rounds of tequila shots on the rooftop bar of the Blue Chairs Hotel.

Zane's pals had been overjoyed to see their best friend suddenly appear out of nowhere. As they drank and reminisced over the good old days, Zane grew uncharacteristically silent.

Feeling like something was seriously wrong; Lumpy quickly asked his friend if everything was alright. Zane nodded numbly and forced down another shot. He wanted to fill his friends in on his dreadful predicament but being powerless to alter the situation; he kept his dark secret to himself.

Trying to regaining a cheerful mood, Zane raised his bottle and halfheartedly proclaimed, *"To my only true friends in the world."*

Slim seemed disturbed by the stoic words, and Lumpy felt the dark vibe as well. To boost Zane's spirit, Slim added another toast. *"Here's to the Tres Desperados! All for one and one for all!"*

After the toast, Zane asked his friends if he could spend some time alone to clear his thoughts. Lumpy shrugged, saying, *" Sure my friend. Me and Slim need to get our beauty sleep anyway!"* With hesitant laughs all-around, the two ex-cons slowly departed, well aware that Zane had some serious issues to deal with.

When Lumpy and Slim had retired to one of the rooms in the Hotel, Zane sat in silence, trying to cope with the illuminating effects of the potent agave brew. When a wave of remorse started to wash-over him, he reflected back on his skewed life.

Before he had initiated his harebrained money scheme, Zane had been a somewhat lackadaisical yet carefree man. He had no entanglements or obligations and had been satisfied with the average yet lackluster person that he was. In hind sight, he wished he had never started the counterfeiting scheme. To be certain, only one good thing came from all his dealings with Lesal Spurnell.

After the life shattering series of encounters with his nemesis and reliving the crazy series of misadventures to elude his terrifying tracker, he had discovered an entirely different person buried within.

He was no longer an aimless and underachieving do-nothing. He had broken out of his former timid shell and had discovered a new zest for living. If it had not been for Axel Gilan's unforeseen intervention, he would have spent the remainder of his days living life without a worry in the world.

As he had performed his detestable duties as an assassin, Zane felt a dark and malicious bubble slowly rising to the surface of his conscience. The joy and peace that he had once desired no longer seemed relevant. After spending many months as a mob hitman, he felt completely cold and barren inside. Nothing in his new life seemed to bring him any reward or delight.

Once gracious and considerate to his friends, his mannerisms had become loutish and abrasive. Zane was constantly agitated by the common people that surrounded him, and he spurned his own existence. It was a painful twist in his life that he could have never predicted.

Feeling utterly soulless and fatalistic, he had finally concluded that nothing in life ended well.

As the first rays of dawn revealed salmon-hued ripples of water over the expansive bay, he stood up suddenly. A compelling vision had exploded from within his tortured mind.

With the muted rumblings of a distant thunderstorm echoing ominously across the mist-covered mountain sides, Zane proclaimed his coldhearted revelation to the world.

Glaring angrily beyond the hazy horizon, he vowed, *"Lesal Spurnell, I swear to God above to take my vengeance upon you. No matter how long it takes, I will comb the earth relentlessly until I flush out your disgusting, overstuffed hide."*

"When I find you, I will torment you unmercifully until you beg like a dog for your death. I will make you suffer in unimaginable agony for what you have done to me. You will pay dearly for destroying my life".

"When my unquenchable craving for retribution is completely satisfied, I will slice up your blubbery carcass into pieces with a chainsaw, and stuff your putrid remains into a guiled box. Then, with a smile of satisfaction, I will ship your worthless corpse to Axel Gilan with my compliments."

"Now, let the games begin."

Once Zane's violent explosion of rage started to subside, he began to sob deeply. His heart suddenly seized with unbearable anguish, and acerbic tears of self-pity flooded his eyes. All-consumed with remorse, he slowly realized that an unfathomable metamorphosis had taken place.

In a perverse reversal of fate, he had been cruelly transformed into the loathsome subhuman he despised most of all.

The End

Lightning Source UK Ltd.
Milton Keynes UK
UKHW011844071220
374768UK00010B/793/J